格雷的老爸

格雷的哥哥
——罗德里克

格雷的"死党"
——罗利

格雷的弟弟
——曼尼

格雷梦想中
的小狗

DIARY of a Wimpy Kid

小屁孩日记⑧

——"头盖骨摇晃机"的幸存者

[美] 杰夫·金尼 著

陈万如 译

格雷的老妈

格雷

·广州·

广东省出版集团

新世纪出版社

本书简体中文版由美国 Harry N. Abrams 公司通过中国 Creative Excellence Rights Agency 独家授权

版权合同登记号：19-2010-058 号

图书在版编目（CIP）数据

小屁孩日记⑧："头盖骨摇晃机"的幸存者/（美）杰夫·金尼著；
陈万如译. —广州：新世纪出版社，2011.1
ISBN 978-7-5405-4459-1

Ⅰ. 小… Ⅱ.①杰… ②陈… Ⅲ. 漫画-作品集-美国-现代 Ⅳ.①J238.2

中国版本图书馆 CIP 数据核字（2010）第 224984 号

出 版 人：陈锐军
选题策划：林 铨 王小斌
责任编辑：王小斌 招海萍
责任技编：王建慧

小屁孩日记⑧
——"头盖骨摇晃机"的幸存者

〔美〕杰夫·金尼 著 陈万如 译

出版发行：新世纪出版社
（广州市大沙头四马路10号 邮政编码：510102）

经 销：全国新华书店
印 刷：广东省教育厅教育印刷厂
开 本：890mm×1240mm 1/32
印 张：7 字 数：150 千字
版 次：2011 年 1 月第 1 版
印 次：2011 年 1 月第 1 次印刷
书 号：ISBN 978-7-5405-4459-1
定 价：14.90 元

质量监督电话：020-83797655 购书咨询电话：020-83793749

有趣的书，好玩的书

夏 致

    这是一个美国中学男生的日记。他为自己的瘦小个子而苦恼，老是会担心被同班的大块头欺负，会感慨"为什么分班不是按个头分而是按年龄分"。这是他心里一道小小的自卑，可是另一方面呢，他又为自己的脑瓜比别人灵光而沾沾自喜，心里嘲笑同班同学是笨蛋，老想投机取巧偷懒。

    他在老妈的要求下写日记，幻想着自己成名后拿日记本应付蜂拥而至的记者；

    他特意在分班时装得不会念书，好让自己被分进基础班，打的主意是"尽可能降低别人对你的期望值，这样即使最后你可能几乎什么都不用干，也总能给他们带来惊喜"；

    他喜欢玩电子游戏，可是他爸爸常常把他赶出家去，好让他多活动一下。结果他跑到朋友家里去继续打游戏，然后在回家的路上用别人家的喷水器弄湿身子，扮成一身大汗的样子；

    他眼红自己的好朋友手受伤以后得到女生的百般呵护，就故意用绷带把自己的手掌缠得严严实实的装伤员，没招来女生的关注反而惹来自己不想搭理的人；

不过，一山还有一山高，格雷再聪明，在家里还是敌不过哥哥罗德里克，还是被耍得团团转；而正在上幼儿园的弟弟曼尼可以"恃小卖小"，无论怎么捣蛋都有爸妈护着，让格雷无可奈何。

这个狡黠、机趣、自恋、胆小、爱出风头、喜欢懒散的男孩，一点都不符合人们心目中的那种懂事上进的好孩子形象，奇怪的是这个缺点不少的男孩子让我忍不住喜欢他。

人们总想对生活中的一切事情贴上个"好"或"坏"的标签。要是找不出它的实在可见的好处，它就一定是"坏"，是没有价值的。单纯的有趣，让我们增添几分好感和热爱，这难道不是比读书学习考试重要得多的事情吗?! 生活就像一个蜜糖罐子，我们是趴在桌子边踮高脚尖伸出手，眼巴巴地瞅着罐子的孩子。有趣不就是蜂蜜的滋味吗？

翻开这本书后，我每次笑声与下一次笑声之间停顿不超过五分钟。一是因为格雷满脑子的鬼主意和诡辩，实在让人忍俊不禁。二是因为我还能毫不费劲地明白他的想法，一下子就捕捉到格雷的逻辑好笑在哪里，然后会心一笑。

小学二年级的时候我和同班的男生打架；初一的时候放学后我在黑板上写"某某某（男生）是个大笨蛋"；初二的时候，同桌的男生起立回答老师的提问，我偷偷移开他的椅子，让他的屁股结结实实地亲吻了地面……我对初中男生的记忆少得可怜。到了高中，进了一所重点中学，大多数男生要么是专心学习的乖男孩，要么是个性飞扬的早熟少年。除了愚人节和邻班的同学集体调换教室糊弄老师以外，男生们很少再玩恶作剧了。仿佛大家不约而同都知道，自己已经过了有资格耍小聪明，并且耍完以后别人会觉得自己可爱的年龄了。

如果你是一位超过中学年龄的大朋友，欢迎你和我在阅读时光中做一次短暂的童年之旅；如果你是格雷的同龄人，我真羡慕你们，因为你们读了这本日记之后，还可以在自己的周围发现比格雷的经历更妙趣横生的小故事，让阅读的美好体验延续到生活里。

要是给我一个机会再过一次童年，我一定会睁大自己还没有患上近视的眼睛，仔细发掘身边有趣的小事情，拿起笔记录下来。亲爱的读者，不知道当你读完这本小书后，是否也有同样的感觉？

片刻之后我转念一想，也许从现在开始，还来得及呢。作者创作这本图画日记那年是 30 岁，那么说来我还有 9 年时间呢。

我这么酷的人竟然也被叫成
"小·屁孩"，真是@＃％＆＊……

星期六

今天早上老妈格外兴奋，我一眼就能看出她有所图谋。

到了10点钟，她叫我们都往旅行车上坐。我问她要去哪儿，她说这是个"惊喜"。

老妈在旅行车后座放了防晒霜和泳衣，我以为这回一定是去海滩。

不过我问老妈的时候，老妈说我们要去的地方比海滩还棒。

姑且不管要去哪里，路上就花了很长时间。跟罗德里克和曼尼一起困在车后厢可不是好玩的。

曼尼坐在我和罗德里克之间凸起的位子上。罗德里克跟曼尼说，曼尼坐的是车上最糟糕的位置，因为那儿最小、最不舒服。

这下好了，曼尼开始大吵大闹。

最后，老妈和老爸实在烦透了曼尼的哭闹。老妈说轮到我坐中间了，因为我是家里第二小的孩子，这才公平。于是每次车碾过马路上的坑洼时，我的头就会撞到车顶。

下午两点钟左右的时候我快饿死了，我问爸妈能不能停车买点快餐。老爸不肯停车，他说快餐店的服务员都是"白痴"。

我当然知道他为什么会这么说。每次老爸光顾我家附近的炸鸡店时，他总是把垃圾箱当作下单处。

我看到一家比萨店的招牌，求老爸老妈让我们在那里吃饭。

不过大概老妈想省钱，因为她已准备好吃的东西了。

半小·时后我们的车停在一个大停车场上。我知道这是什么地方了。

这是激流冲浪水上乐园，这个地方我们小·时候来过。我说的是我小·不丁点的时候。

这种地方是给曼尼这么大的人去的。

老妈准是听到了我和罗德里克在后座唉声叹气。她说我们一家人会玩得尽兴，今天会是我们这个暑假的高潮。

我对激流冲浪水上乐园的回忆很糟糕。有一次爷爷带我来，把我扔在水上滑梯区一整天。他说他要读书，三小·时后在那里等我。但我几乎一个水上滑梯都没玩，因为入口的告示牌写着：

48" 以下
须有成人陪同

我以为要到 48 岁才可以玩，后来才知道数字后面两小·撇原来是"英寸"的意思。

所以我一直在等爷爷回来接我，一整天时间就这样白白过去，然后我们就回家了。

罗德里克对水上乐园的回忆也很糟糕。去年有人请他的乐队到冲浪池附近的舞台表演。罗德里克的乐队要求水上乐园的工作人员摆放一台烟雾机，为表演增加一点特殊效果。

但事情弄砸了，对方给了乐队一台泡泡制造机。

我知道老妈为什么今天带我们来水上乐园——家庭票半价优惠。倒霉的是，好像全美国的家庭都跑来这里玩了。

我们买票进门，老妈给曼尼租了一架手推车。我说服老妈多花点钱租了架双人手推车，我知道今天会过得很漫长，我得保存体力。

老妈把手推车放在冲浪池旁边。冲浪池人山人海，几乎看不到水面。我们刚抹上防晒霜，找了个可以坐下来的地方，我就感觉到几滴雨水落下来，接着雷声轰鸣。这时候，广播宣布了一个通知。

由于闪电天气，水上乐园现在停止营业。感谢您的光临，祝您生活愉快！

人们争先恐后地往出口赶，找到自己的车子就跳上去。所有人都想立刻离开，于是形成了一条壮观的车龙。

曼尼想说笑话逗大家笑。起初老爸老妈挺捧他的场。

但是，过了一会儿，曼尼的笑话就令人不敢恭维了。

车子所剩的汽油不多了，我们只好关上空调，等待前面的车子先驶出停车场。

老妈说她头疼，到车后厢躺下了。一个小时后，停车场的车龙终于消失了，我们驶上了高速公路。

我们在路上一个加油站加了油，四十五分钟后我们就到家了。老爸让我叫醒老妈，我往旅行车后厢一看，糟了！老妈不见了！

大家想了好几分钟，也没人能搞懂老妈去哪了。后来我们反应过来了——她只可能在加油站。她准是趁停车的机会上厕所，可我们都没有注意到她下车了。

果不其然，回到加油站一看，她就在那儿。看到老妈我们很高兴，不过我想老妈见到我们时是不会太开心的。

在回家的路上，老妈一声不吭。直觉告诉我，家庭团聚活动老妈已经受够了。这是好事，因为我也受够了。

星期日

要是昨天我们没有去水上乐园玩那该多好啊。那样我们可以呆在家里，我的鱼就不会离开人世了。

出门之前我喂了鱼，老妈说我应该把罗德里克的鱼也喂了。罗德里克把鱼养在冰箱顶上的玻璃鱼缸里，我敢说罗德里克从来都没喂过他的鱼，也没清洗过鱼缸。

我估计，罗德里克的鱼大概是靠吃玻璃表面长出来的海藻活下来的。

啧吧 啧吧

老妈一看到罗德里克的鱼缸，就大呼"恶心"。然后她把他的鱼倒进了我的鱼缸里。

从水上乐园回到家，我就直奔厨房去喂鱼。可我的鱼已经不在了，无需多想就知道发生了什么事。

我甚至连悲伤的时间都没有，因为今天是父亲节，我们一家人得开车去爷爷家吃午饭。

我跟你说，如果我哪一天做了父亲，你绝对不会在父亲节那天看到我整整齐齐穿着衬衣打着领带去老人活动中心。我会一个人找乐子。不过老妈说，看到赫夫利一家三代聚在一起，感觉真好。

　　我准是一直在用手里的叉子把食物拨来拨去，因为老爸问我食物有什么问题。我跟他说，我的鱼死了，我很伤心。老爸说他不知道该怎么安慰我，因为他没经历过宠物去世的事。

　　老爸说他小时候养过一条狗，叫"果仁儿"，不过后来"果仁儿"跑到一个叫蝴蝶农场的地方，就再也没回来。

　　这个"果仁儿和蝴蝶农场"的故事我可以倒背如流，但我不想让自己显得没礼貌，就没有打断老爸的话。

　　这时候爷爷说话了，他说自己要"忏悔"。他说"果仁儿"并没有跑到蝴蝶农场，实际上是有一次他在家门前倒车，不小心把狗碾死了。

爷爷说，为了瞒住老爸，他特意编了蝴蝶农场的故事，以为现在他们两父子可以为此一笑泯恩仇了。

没想到，老爸气坏了。他立刻叫我们上车，扔下爷爷和午饭的账单不管就开车走了。一路上老爸一言不发。到家后他让我们下车，又开车一溜烟儿走了。

老爸去了很长一段时间。我开始想这一天他是不是要自个儿找乐子。不过一个小时后老爸带着一个大纸箱回来了。

老爸把纸箱放在地上，哇！里面居然有只小狗！

老爸擅自作主买了一只狗回来，老妈看起来不怎么激动，在这之前，老爸连给自己买条短裤都要事先征得老妈的同意。不过看到老爸高兴的样子，老妈也就给他开绿灯了。

晚饭时老妈说，该给小狗取个名字。

我想给它取个"绞肉机"或者"尖牙王"之类听起来很酷的名字，不过老妈说这些名字太"暴力"。

曼尼的提议比我的更糟糕。他想给小狗取"大象"或者"斑马"之类的动物名字。

罗德里克喜欢曼尼的提议，他说我们应该把小狗叫做"海龟"。

老妈说我们应该叫小·狗"甜心"。这个主意太糟了，它可是个男孩，不是女孩啊。

但我们还没来得及提出反对意见，老爸已经点头同意了。

简称"阿甜"。

我觉得嘛，只要老妈不叫老爸把小·狗送回去，她说什么老爸都会赞成。不过第六感告诉我，乔叔叔是不会赞成给小·狗取这个名字的。

老爸叫罗德里克去超市买个盛狗粮的平底碗，还要把小·狗的名字印在碗上。于是罗德里克回家的时候就拿个着碗，上面写着——

汗①

看！这就是你让全家拼写最差劲的家伙替你效劳的后果。

星期三

家里养了狗，起初我高兴得不得了，不过现在我得好好考虑一下了。

小·狗最近快把我搞疯了。几天之前，有天晚上电视台播了一则广告，画面上有几只地鼠"呼"的从洞里钻出来，"呼"的又不见了。

阿甜似乎对这些动感画面颇感兴趣，于是老爸说——

① 在英文中"sweaty"（汗涔涔的）和"sweetie"（甜心、宝贝）的读音相近。

13

阿甜被老爸搞烦了，冲着电视"汪汪"叫。

现在阿甜总是冲着电视狂叫，只有地鼠的广告能让他安静下来。

不过最让我闹心的是小狗喜欢在我的床上睡觉，我很害怕抱走他的时候他会一口咬掉我的手。

而且他不光是睡在我的床上那么简单，他还要睡在床的正中央。

老爸每天早上7点都进我的房间带阿甜出去。我觉得我和小·狗有个共同点，同样不喜欢一大早起床。于是为了叫醒小狗，老爸每天都反复开关电灯。

昨天老爸用这种方法叫不动阿甜，就用了新办法。他去前门按门铃，小狗一听到铃声就像火箭一样飘了出去。

唯一的问题是，他把我的脸当做了发射台。

今天早上准是下雨了，因为阿甜从外面回来后浑身湿透直发抖。他拼命想钻进我的被窝取暖。幸好我为了防范泥手①做了很多准备工作，足以把小狗挡住。

星期四

今天早上老爸使尽浑身解数也没把小狗从我的床上唤起来，只好上班去了。大概过了一小时，阿甜弄醒了我，让我带他到外面去。我用毯子紧紧裹住身体开了前门让他出去，等他干完事再自己回来。不料阿甜决意要，出去撒欢儿，我只好跟着他跑。

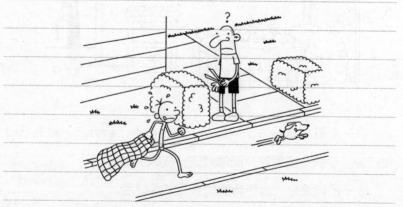

① 《小屁孩日记7——从天而降的巨债》里提到的一部恐怖影片里的一只手，会到处游走、杀人，给格雷造成了很大的心理阴影。

16

你要知道，阿甜还没来我家的时候，这个暑假我一直过得挺滋润。它一来，破坏了对我来说最重要的两件事：看电视和睡眠。

我整天赖在床上，老爸总是看我不爽，而阿甜的贪睡程度是我的两倍，可老爸就是爱他爱得发疯。

但我认为这不是两情相悦。老爸总想让小·狗亲一下他的鼻子，阿甜就是不肯就范。

扭来扭去

蹬腿

我能理解小·狗为什么不喜欢老爸。

抖抖

尽管老妈很少理会阿甜，可他真正喜欢的人只有老妈一个。看得出，这种情况让老爸有点抓狂。

我想阿甜是个容易被女性吸引的男生，所以我们又多了一个共同点。

六月

星期六

昨晚我在创作能够取代"可爱丽儿"的新漫画。这次公开征稿应该会有很多人来竞争，我希望我的作品可以鹤立鸡群。我这个叫"嘿，人们！"的作品有点半漫画半专栏的味道。我觉得这幅漫画可以让世界变得更美好，或者至少让我的世界变得更美好。

想到老爸也看漫画连载，我最好也专门针对他画几幅画。

本来我昨晚可以画不少幅漫画的，都怪阿甜在捣乱，搞到我无法集中精神。

我在画画，他就坐在我的枕头上舔爪子和尾巴，一脸投入状。

每次阿甜这样，我就得提醒自己睡觉时把枕头翻过来睡。昨天晚上我一时大意忘了，结果我一躺下来头就靠在湿漉漉的枕头上。

说到舔爪子，昨晚阿甜终于亲了老爸一下。很可能是因为老爸呼出的气体有番茄薯片味。我觉得狗对这种味道有种本能的反应。

舔

我没有胆量跟老爸说，告诉他前半个小时阿甜一直坐在我的枕头上舔自己的屁股。

不管怎么样，我希望自己今晚可以多画几幅漫画，因为我明天没法开工。明天是独立日①，老妈安排我们一家去镇上的公共游泳池。

我想脱身，主要是因为我想平安度过这个暑假，不想再看到那些五大三粗的老男人洗澡。但老妈还是希望这个暑假能有一个完美的家庭同乐日，所以我反抗也没有用。

星期一

独立日一开始我就很不顺。到了游泳场，我以最快的速度走过更衣室。但那些洗澡的家伙多嘴多舌，并没有放过我。

---

① 每年的7月4日是美国庆祝国家从英国殖民地独立的日子，全国休假。

20

老妈说她把太阳眼镜落在车里了，所以我得从沐浴区折回到停车场。我戴着老妈的眼镜，以清楚表明我没兴趣跟他们搭话，不过这也没起什么作用。

说认真的，我真希望这些老男人在家里洗过澡再来游泳场。因为你一旦见过那种模样的人，你就再也不想再看到他们。

穿过更衣室后的情况也好不到哪里去。眼前人山人海的场景跟我记忆中的一模一样，甚至比以前更加拥挤。大概所有人的想法都一样，要在游泳池度过独立日。

教生员需要定时休息十五分钟，这时全部小孩都要从水池上来。只有这个时候泳池才会腾空。

我觉得救生员休息的目的是给大人一点时间享用泳池，可我想知道在三百多个小孩虎视眈眈等着下水的情况下，那些大人怎么能游得自在。

几年前我还小，救生员休息的时候我就去婴儿池游泳，但我看到那里的一幕后，就再也没去了。

妈妈，我在尿尿！

泳池唯一一个人少的地方是深水区，跳板就在那里。八岁那一年罗德里克花言巧语骗我上跳板去跳水，以后我再也没去过深水区。

那时候，罗德里克一直处心积虑哄我上去跳水，不过我被高高的梯子吓住了。他跟我说，要克服自己内心的恐惧，否则永远都成不了男子汉。

后来有一天，罗德里克跟我说跳板上面有个小丑在派免费玩具，我一下就被吸引住了。

等我意识到罗德里克说的全是一派胡言的时候，已经来不及了。

言归正传，今天老妈叫我们一起去野餐区，因为今天在那里可以免费吃西瓜。

可我对西瓜也有恐惧症。罗德里克总是跟我说，要是你吞下西瓜籽，你的胃就会长出西瓜来。

我不晓得他说的是不是实话，不过没几个月就开学了，我不想冒这个险。

天慢慢黑了，大家都在草坪上铺开厚布，准备欣赏焰火表演。我们坐在草坪上，直直地盯着天空好一段时间，却什么都没有看到。

没多久有人用扩音器说话，他说由于昨晚有工作人员忘了把烟花搬进屋里，烟花被雨淋湿了，演出取消。有些小孩哭了，于是有几个大人想自己来搞一场焰火表演。

幸运的是，就在这时南边的乡村俱乐部开始放焰火。视线要越过树顶有点困难，不过这时候大概没有谁会在乎这点小麻烦。

星期二

今天早上我坐在餐桌边上翻报纸看漫画，看得我差点吐出口里的燕麦片。

报纸上最显眼的地方登了一则两版大的开学广告。

还有两个月才开学，这时候登载开学广告居然合法，简直难以置信。能做出这种事情的人保准一点也不喜欢小孩。

我肯定开学广告从现在开始逐渐从各处冒出来，然后呢，老妈就要告诉我该去买衣服了。和老妈去购物就得耗上一整天。

我问老妈可不可以改成由老爸带我去买衣服，她说行。我估计她以为这是一个培养父子感情的机会。

不过我跟老爸说他可以一个人去，爱买啥就买啥。

这个提议真是蠢到家了，因为所有东西老爸都在药店里买。

看到那则开学广告之前，我的日子已经够糟了。今天早上天又下雨，老爸带了阿甜上街，它回家后又猛钻我的被窝。

我准是有点心不在焉，因为这狗在被子和床之间找到一个空档，钻了进来。

听我说，没有什么事比困在被窝里、只穿着内裤，有只湿漉漉的狗在你身上爬来爬去更恐怖的了。

就在我为狗和开学广告闹心的时候，这一天的生活发生了大逆转。老妈冲印了几张独立日那天拍的照片，照片摊在餐桌上没有收起来。

从其中一张照片上你可以看到背景有个救生员。尽管看出救生员是谁有点困难。不过我很肯定那是希瑟·希尔斯。

昨天游泳场人山人海，我压根没注意救生员长啥样。如果真的是希瑟·希尔斯，我简直不敢相信自己竟然和她擦身而过。

希瑟·希尔斯是荷莉·希尔斯的姐姐，荷莉是我们班上最可爱的女生之一。希瑟上高中了，那跟初中比可是截然不同的江湖。

荷莉·希尔斯　　　　　希瑟·希尔斯

希瑟·希尔斯的出现彻底改变了我对小镇游泳场的看法。我开始重新审视整个暑假。那只狗已经摧毁了我呆在家里的所有乐趣，要是不尽快行动，这个暑假就没有什么好事可以说的了。

汪汪 汪汪 汪汪

所以从明天开始，我要以全新的态度投入生活。希望到开学的时候，我也能有一个读高中的女朋友。

星期三

老妈今天很高兴，因为我愿意跟着她和曼尼一起去游泳场。她说她为我感动和自豪，说我终于把自己的家庭看得比电子游戏重要了。我没有跟老妈提起希瑟·希尔斯，我不想让她知道我愿意和她们去游泳场是因为她的缘故，我也不需要她插足我的感情生活。

小镇
游泳场

到了泳场，我想直奔泳池，看看希瑟是不是在值班。不过我意识到，最好还是做好她在现场的充分准备。

于是我到洗手间给自己充充电，往身上抹防晒油。接着又做了好几个俯卧撑和仰卧起坐，好让我的肌肉鼓起来。

我在洗手间大概呆了十五分钟。就在我在镜子面前检查个人形象的时候，一个隔间中传出有人清喉咙的声音。

这下子，丢脸丢到家了，给里面那个人看到我在镜子前做的各种动作。搞不好那个人跟我一样，要等所有人都离开了才能在马桶上干事。

我估计隔间里的人看不到我的脸，所以至少他不会知道我是谁。我正要偷偷溜出洗手间，老妈突然在男更衣室门口喊话。

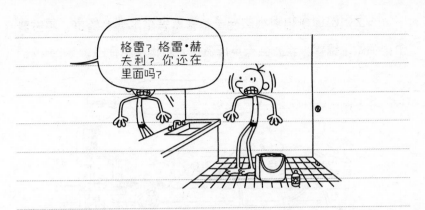

老妈问我在里面呆了那么久干啥，为什么看起来"容光焕发"，不过我的视线已经越过她，扫视着救生员的座位，看希瑟·希尔斯在不在上面。

果然，她就在那里。我径直朝她走去，在她的椅子下面附近站住。

每隔一阵子我就说几句俏皮话，我觉得自己一定会给她留下深刻印象。

一看到她像是想喝水的样子，我就会给她端一杯水。每次哪个孩子做了错事，我就会大声斥责他，省得希瑟开口。

每当希瑟看守某个位置的时间结束，我都会随她到她的下一个救生员座位。到了第四次换位置的时候，我刚好坐在老妈前面。听我说，当你老妈在你身后两米的地方坐着，你就会感到如芒在背似的。

我真希望希瑟知道我愿意为她做任何事。要是她想有人帮着把防晒油抹到她背上，或者她想在跳下水后上岸时有人用大毛巾包着她，我就是那个人。

我一直跟着希瑟绕着泳场转，直到泳场停止营业时才离开。回家的路上我在想，要是我余下的假期都像今天这样过，正如老妈说的那样，今年的暑假一定会是人生最美好的暑假。唯一一样会摧毁这一切的东西是那只可恶的泥手。我肯定它会在最关键的时候出现，坏了我的好事。

星期三

过去一周我每天都和希瑟呆在一起。

如果我把我和希瑟之间的故事说给学校的朋友听，他们永远不会相信。于是我站在救生员座位的旁边，叫老妈给我拍一张照片。

老妈没有带她自己的照相机，就用了她的手机拍。可她搞不清怎样用手机拍照，我像傻瓜一样站了好长一段时间。

最后我总算教会老妈按下正确的按钮拍照了，可她按下按钮的时候，镜头对错了位置，她给自己拍了照。看到了吧，这就是我一直说新科技在成人那里是暴殄天物的原因了。

我教老妈用镜头对着我，可就在那时候，她的电话响了，她接了电话。

老妈聊了五分钟左右的电话，等她挂了电话的时候，希瑟已经在她的下一个座位上。可老妈不管三七二十一照样给我拍照。

咔嚓

星期五

　　靠老妈开车送我去游泳池开始成了问题。老妈不想每天去游泳，而且即使她去，她也只是去几个小时。

　　而我则想守在泳池边上，从它开门迎客到闭门谢客为止，这样子我和希瑟呆在一起的时间最长。我不打算叫罗德里克开他的小货车载我，因为他总是要我坐后厢，那里又没有座椅。

　　我知道我得靠自己解决交通问题，我很幸运，昨天找到了解决办法。

　　不知哪个邻居在路边放了一辆自行车，我抢在其他人之前把自行车拿走。

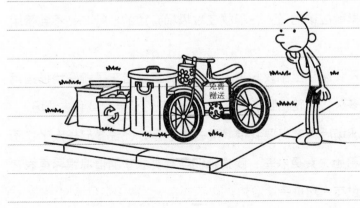

我把自行车骑回家，停在车库里。老爸看到自行车，说那是一辆"女式车"，我应该扔了它。

你先听我说，女式车至少有两方面比男式车好。第一，女式车的座垫又大又软，你穿着泳裤骑车的时候这一点很重要。

第二，女式车的车头有篮子，可以放电子游戏光盘盒和防晒油。而且，我的自行车还有个车铃，用起来那叫一个方便！

星期一

我早就应该知道，一辆放在垃圾桶旁边的自行车是不会管用很久的。

昨天我从家里出发骑车去泳场，骑着骑着车子就开始摇摇晃晃。没多久，前轮松脱了。所以今天我只好请老妈载我去泳场。

到泳场后，老妈要我带曼尼去更衣室。她说曼尼长大了，不能再跟着她去女更衣室。我猜她们在女更衣室的情况跟男更衣室一样，也有人光身子淋浴。

本来带曼尼从更衣室一端走到另一端只用五秒钟。但我们用了十分钟。

曼尼到哪里都是跟着老妈，在此之前他从来没去过男洗手间。他好奇心大发，看到什么东西都想去弄一下。我一度阻止他在小便器里洗手，我想他一定是把小便器当成了洗手池。

我不想让曼尼经过淋浴区时看见我曾经见过的一幕。于是我从提包里掏出一条毛巾，准备在我们经过淋浴区的时候盖住曼尼的眼睛。可就在我从包里掏毛巾的那一瞬间，曼尼一下就跑开不见了。你绝对想不到他去了哪儿。

我知道我得营救曼尼，于是我紧闭双眼，走进去救他。

我生怕自己会触到那些正在淋浴的家伙，有一刹那我以为自己碰到了。

我只好睁开眼睛找曼尼，我一把抓住他，飞一般地逃出去。

我们到更衣室出口的时候，曼尼看起来挺精神的，可我觉得自己还没能从刚才噩梦般的情况中恢复过来。

我的据点在希瑟的救生员座位下方。我跌跌撞撞地走到那里坐下来，然后开始深呼吸，让自己平静下来。

五分钟过后，有个小孩在希瑟的座位后面吐了，准是吃了太多冰淇淋。希瑟回头看了一眼，然后往下看，好像她在等我去做些什么。我想高尚的做法是帮希瑟清理地上的呕吐物，不过这实在是超过了我个人使命的需要。

不管怎么说，最近我作了一番深入思考，我意识到自己需要稍稍冷处理一下这段夏日爱情了。

况且希瑟明年都上大学了，那些异地恋也没见过多少对能成功的。

八月

星期二

今天我们在超市遇上杰弗逊一家。我和罗利已经一个多月没跟对方说过话了，所以场面有点尴尬。

杰弗逊太太说他们正在为下周的海滩之旅采购食物。一听这话我怒了，因为那本来是我们家这个暑假要去的地方。不过杰弗逊太太后面的一句话更让我大吃一惊。

让格雷和我们一起去玩怎么样？

杰弗逊先生似乎不大赞成这个提议，不过他还没来得及说什么，老妈已经接过话头。

好啊，格雷肯定很乐意！

这件事我总觉得有点不可思议。我在想老妈和杰弗逊太太是不是合谋让我和罗利和好，而这只是个开场？

相信我，罗利是我最不想和他共度一个星期的人。但后来我意识到，要是我跟着杰弗逊一家去海滩，我就可以玩"头盖骨摇晃机"。那我这个暑假到最后也许不会过得那么失败。

星期一

到了这地方一看，我就知道跟他们来海滩玩是大错特错了。

我们家每次都是在木板道附近高高的地方租一间公寓房住，但杰弗逊家住的地方是离海滩五公里远的一间小木屋。木屋里面既没有电视，也没有电脑，什么带屏幕的东西都没有。

我问他们有什么可以玩，杰弗逊太太说：

有本书你可以看看！

我还以为是什么好书，正准备跟罗利说他妈妈真有趣的时候，杰弗逊太太回来了。她拿着好几本阅读材料。

　　这样一来就更加可以确定，老妈一开始就参与了整个计划。

　　杰弗逊一家三个人都在读书，一直读到吃饭时间。晚饭味道还行，不过甜品太糟糕了。杰弗逊太太就是那些偷偷往你的零食里夹带健康食品的母亲，她做的布朗尼蛋糕里全是菠菜。

　　我觉得把蔬菜磨碎后放在小孩的甜品里不是什么好点子，因为这样一来他们就不会知道真正的甜品是什么味道了。

　　罗利第一次吃正常的布朗尼蛋糕是在我们家。说真的，当时的情况很难堪。

　　晚饭过后，杰弗逊太太叫我们一起去客厅玩游戏。我心里希望是玩些扑克之类的正常游戏，但杰弗逊家对"有趣"有自己的理解。

杰弗逊一家玩一个叫"我爱你是因为……"的游戏，轮到我的时候我弃权了。

然后我们玩猜字谜，轮到罗利的时候，他扮的是狗。

9点左右，杰弗逊先生叫我们上床睡觉。这时候我才发现木屋里的睡觉设施比娱乐设施还要糟糕。

房间里只有一张床，我跟罗利说我们可以做个交易：我们扔硬币决定，谁睡床上，另一个人就睡地上。

可罗利往硬邦邦、乱糟糟的地毯上看了一眼，说他不想冒险。我也决定不去睡地板。于是我和罗利一起睡床上，但尽量和他保持距离。

罗利没多久就鼾声如雷，可我半边身子悬在空中，怎么也睡不着。最后我终于迷迷糊糊有点睡意，这时罗利又突然尖叫起来，好像他受到了袭击一样。

有那么一瞬间我以为我们被泥手攥住了。

罗利的爸妈赶紧跑进来，看看发生了什么事。

44

罗利说他做噩梦了，梦到有只小鸡藏在他的身下。

接下来的二十分钟，罗利爸妈都在哄他安静下来，跟他说那只是一个噩梦而已，真的没有小鸡。

没人操心我，关心我从床上脸朝地摔下来之后怎么样了。

罗利这一晚睡在他爸妈的房间里，这最好不过。少了罗利和他的小鸡梦打扰我睡觉，我可以美美地睡一觉了。

星期三

到了今天我已经被困在这间小木屋里三天了，我真的要发疯了。

我一直努力让杰弗逊夫妇带我们去木板道上玩，可他们却说那里太"嘈杂"了。

我从来没有经历过这么长时间没有电视、电脑和电子游戏的生活，我开始觉得有点绝望了。趁杰弗逊先生熬夜用手提电脑工作的时候，我偷偷下楼看他上网，好看一看外面的世界。

我求了杰弗逊先生好几次，求他让我用用手提电脑，可他说那是他的"工作电脑"，不想被我搞坏。昨天晚上我快要崩溃了，于是我冒了个小小的险。

一看到杰弗逊先生从椅子起来去上厕所，我马上抓住机会。

我以最快的速度匆匆写了一封电子邮件给老妈，然后跑上楼跳上床。

收件人：赫夫利·苏珊
主题：紧急求救
救命 救命 把我带出这里 这几个人快把我逼疯了

今天早上我下楼准备吃早餐，没想到杰弗逊先生一脸不悦地看着我。

原来我是用了杰弗逊先生的工作账户发的邮件，老妈还回复了。

收件人：杰弗逊·罗伯特
主题：回复：紧急求救
家庭旅行有时候很考验人！格雷不乖吗？
苏珊

我以为杰弗逊会狠狠教训我一顿，可他什么也没说。这时候杰弗逊太太说，不如下午晚点时候我们去木板道玩一两个小时。

哈，这正是我一直希望的事情。给我几个小时就足够了。

要是我可以玩一次"头盖骨摇晃机"，我就会觉得这次出门完全没有白来。

星期五

我比原计划提前两天回家，这原因么，说来话长。

杰弗逊两口子昨天下午带我和罗利去木板道玩。我一心想着第一件事就是玩"头盖骨摇晃机"，不过排队的人太多了，所以我们打算去买点食物，晚点再来。

我们四个人都买了冰淇淋，但杰弗逊太太只给我们买了一个冰淇淋筒。

出门前老妈给了我三十块钱，一个嘉年华游戏就花了我二十块。

我想赢一个巨型毛毛虫毛绒玩具回家，不过我觉得这游戏一定有猫腻，让你永远也赢不了。

罗利看着我扔掉了二十块钱，然后就叫他爸爸到旁边一家商店给他买一个一模一样的巨型毛毛虫毛绒玩具，只花了十块钱，可把我气坏了。

杰弗逊先生这么做实在是大错特错。现在罗利以为自己是个赢家，可他明明不是嘛。

我自己对此深有体会。去年我还在游泳队的时候，有一个星期他们邀请我去参加一个特别游泳聚会。

我到了现场一看，哪有什么游泳冠军。一帮从未获得过任何奖项的小屁孩而已。

起初我还挺开心，说不定这次我可以真的赢一回比赛。

不过我还是表现不佳。我的参赛项目是100米自由式，最后一个来回我都游不动了，只能走完全程。

还好裁判没有判我违规罚我下场。这一晚到了最后，我得了一条冠军绶带，而且颁奖人还是我老爸老妈。

事实上，每个人回家的时候都佩戴着冠军绶带，连仰泳时转身游错泳道的汤米·兰姆也有一条。

回家之后我觉得很疑惑。罗德里克看到我的冠军绶带，便向我透露了其中的内幕。

罗德里克说冠军赛只不过是家长们设的骗局，这样可以让他们的孩子感觉到自己就是冠军。

我估计父母以为自己为孩子做了一件大好事，不过要是你问我，我会说这只是制造了更多问题。

我还记得以前我在儿童棒球队的时候，哪怕我三击未中出局，其他人也会为我欢呼。可到了下一年，我到了少年棒球队。每回我犯了丢高飞球之类的失误，其他队友和他们的家长都会嘘我下场。

我说这些话的意思是，要是罗利父母想让罗利自我感觉良好，他们就不应该仅仅在他小时候才这么做，而长大了就不管他。他们应该一直做下去。

买了毛毛虫玩偶，我们就一直往前走，到了木板道上，排队等着玩"头盖骨摇晃机"。这时候有样东西引起了我的注意。

我看到罗德里克钥匙扣照片上的女孩了，就立在这儿。不过，她不是真人，是纸板人像。

　　我真是个傻瓜，之前怎么会以为照片上的女孩是真有其人。然后我马上意识到，我也可以给自己买个钥匙扣照片，让学校里那帮家伙大吃一惊。我甚至还可以向他们收取观看费，赚上一笔。

　　我付了五块钱，摆好姿势准备拍照。不幸的是，杰弗逊一家挤进了镜头里，所以现在我的纪念钥匙扣是一文不值了。

　　我很生气，不过回头看到"头盖骨摇晃机"的等候队伍只剩几个人，我一高兴就什么又都忘了。我一溜小·跑过去，用我最后的五块钱买了入场票。

　　我以为罗利就在我身后，但他还在我身后十尺远的地方。我猜他是胆小·不敢玩。

　　我开始想需不需要再考虑一下有什么问题，不过一切都晚了。操作员给我拴上安全带后，就把我锁在笼子里，我知道自己不能回头了。

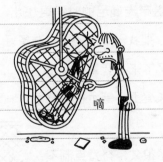

嘀

　　唉，我为什么不花点时间先看看"头盖骨摇晃机"到底对一个人做了啥呢，要是我知道的话，我永远都不会去玩。

　　它让你首尾翻滚无数个来回，然后把你往地上甩，甩到脸离地面只有6英寸的地方。然后呢，又让你快速往天空方向旋转。

　　这期间，装着你的笼子"嘎吱嘎吱"作响，那些螺栓看上去就像马上要松脱下来。我使劲喊工作人员停下来，可在重金属音乐的敲击声中，没人能听见我在喊什么。

那是我一生中最想呕吐的时候。我的意思是，比上回我被迫从公共泳池的淋浴区带走曼尼的时候更想吐。要是做一个男子汉需要经受这种考验，那我一定是还没有准备好。

摇晃机终于停了下来，我晕得几乎走不了路。我坐在长凳上，等木板道停止旋转。

我在长凳上坐了很久，努力克制不让自己吐出来。而罗利就玩一些适合他的速度的游乐项目。

罗利玩完幼稚的游戏，他爸爸就在纪念品商店给他买了一个充气气球、一件上衣。

我是"头盖骨摇晃机"的幸存者

半小时后，我终于歇够了，准备站起来到处走走。但我刚站稳，杰弗逊先生就说我们该走了。

我问他可不可以让我在游戏机室玩几个游戏，尽管他一脸不乐意的表情，但还是说"行"。

老妈给我的钱我已经花光了，所以我跟杰弗逊先生说给我二十块钱就差不多了，但他只愿意给我一块钱。

杰弗逊夫妇可能受不了游戏机室嘈杂的声音，他们不肯进去，让我们自己去玩，十分钟后在外面和他们碰头。

我进了游戏机室最里面，那里放着一台游戏机叫"雷伏特"。去年我花了五十块钱玩这台机，得了最高分。我想让罗利看到我的名字在分数榜上的第一位。我想给他看看真正的胜利是怎么样的，它可不是别人拱手送给你的。

我的名字还在排分数榜的第一位，不过排在第二位的人一定心怀妒意，眼红我的王者地位。

高分榜

1.	格雷·赫夫利
2.	是个笨蛋
3.	锅盖头 7l
4.	鲁莽
5.	胆小鬼
6.	德尔
7.	野狗
8.	敏捷
9.	张三
10.	李四

我拔掉机器的插头，想消除分数记录，但它们已经永久刻在屏幕上。

我正要花钱玩别的游戏，这时候我突然想起罗利跟我说过的一个把戏。我意识到我们可以用这一块钱多玩点时间。

我和罗利走到外面，站在木板道下面。然后我把钞票插在木板之间的缝隙里，静候上钩的第一条"鱼儿"。

终于有一帮小混混发现了木板道上伸出来的钞票。

等有个小混混弯下腰想把钞票捡起来的时候，我在最后一秒把钞票从木板上拉了下来。

我必须把钞票给罗利玩玩，因为这实在太好玩了。

不过被我们戏弄的小·混混很不高兴，他们跟在我们后面。我和罗利拔腿就跑，等我们肯定自己已经甩掉了他们一帮人才敢停下来。

可我还是觉得不安全。我叫罗利耍几招他学到的空手道招式给我看看，我想万一被那帮人发现我们时也能对付他们两下子。

但罗利说他是空手道金带，不会把他的招式教给一个"无带"的人。

我们在下面又躲了一段时间，直到那帮小·混混不见了，到最后我们觉得危险已经过去。这时候我们反应过来了，我们来到了儿童乐园的下面，所以在我们头顶上就有一批批新的钞票游戏上当者。跟这帮小·屁孩玩可比跟那些小·混混玩要好玩得多了。

嘶啦

不过有一个小孩身手了得，我还没来得及拉下钞票他已经把票子揣了起来。于是我和罗利只好走上木板道，去讨回我们的钱。

可那小孩不愿意把钱还给我们。我费尽心思跟他解释什么叫个人财产，可他就是不肯把钞票还给我。

我被这个小孩搞到束手无策，这时候罗利的父母来了。见到他们我相当高兴，要是有人能让这个小孩讲点道理，这个人就是杰弗逊先生。

但杰弗逊先生很生气，我的意思是说他真的很生气。他说他和太太到处找我们，找了一个小时，刚才他们正打算报警说我们失踪了。

接着他叫我们上车。去停车场的路上我们经过游戏机室。我问杰弗逊先生能不能再给我们一块钱去玩，因为我们压根没花他之前给的那一块钱。

但我这个问题可能问错了，因为他一声不吭带我们上了车。

我们回到小·木屋后，杰弗逊先生叫我和罗利直接回房去。真讨厌，当时还不到晚上8点，外面天还亮着。

但杰弗逊先生要我们马上上床睡觉，而且说他在第二天早上之前不想听到我们发出任何声响。

罗利很难受。从他的神情动作来看，似乎以前他和他爸的关系从来没闹过这么僵。

我想让罗利的心情轻松一点，决定跟他开个玩笑。我在粗毛地毯上走来走去，利用静电感应电了罗利一下。

这招似乎让罗利重新振作起来。他绕着圈圈在地毯上走了五分钟，边走边用脚和地毯摩擦，趁我刷牙的时候以牙还牙。

我绝对不能让罗利占我上风，等他上床躺好，我拿了他的大气球，解开粗大的橡皮绑带，让它全速前进。

要是我再这么做一次，也许我不会那么使劲儿。

罗利睁开眼，看到自己手臂上的红印子，吓得大叫起来，我知道这回惹麻烦了。果不其然，不到五秒钟他父母就出现在我们的房间里。

我竭力解释罗利手臂上的红印是橡皮绷带造成的，不过这对杰弗逊一家人来说毫无意义。

他们给我爸妈打电话，两小时后老爸就到了木屋接我回家。

星期一

老爸接我来回花了四小时，他气坏了。老妈却一点没恼。她说这次我和罗利之间的事只不过是"小孩子打打闹闹"，她很高兴我们又成了"亲朋密友"。

可老爸依然很恼火，我们回来以后我和他之间变得很冷淡。老妈一直想让我们一起去看个电影或干点其他事，好让我们"握手言和"。不过我觉得眼下最好还是让我和老爸各行其道。

我觉得老爸糟糕的心情一时半会好不了，部分原因和我一点关系也没有。我翻开几天的报纸，下面是我在"文艺副刊"上看到的内容——

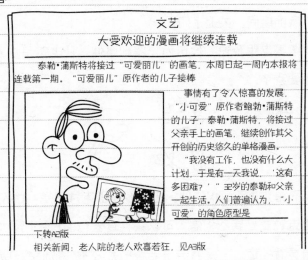

文艺
大受欢迎的漫画将继续连载

泰勒·蒲斯特将接过"可爱丽儿"的画笔，本周日起一周内本报将连载第一期。"可爱丽儿"原作者的儿子接棒。

事情有了令人惊喜的发展，"小·可爱"原作者鲍勃·蒲斯特的儿子，泰勒·蒲斯特，将接过父亲手上的画笔，继续创作其父开创的历史悠久的单格漫画。

"我没有工作，也没有什么大计划，于是有一天我说，'这有多困难？'"王岁的泰勒和父亲一起生活。人们普遍认为，"小·可爱"的角色原型是

下转A2版
相关新闻：老人院的老人欢喜若狂，见A3版

昨天晚上老爸进我房间跟我说话，这是我们三天以来第一次和对方说话。他说他想问清楚周日我在不在家，我说在。

过了一会儿我听到他和别人在聊电话，他的行动有点鬼鬼祟祟。

好……我会给他留足够一星期用的食物和水。

之后我问老爸是不是准备星期天专门带我去哪里玩。这个问题好像让他很不自在。他说不是，不过他不敢直视我的眼睛。

现在我知道老爸没有说真话，于是开始有点担心，因为老爸曾经打定主意要遣送我去军事学校，他没什么干不出来的。

我不知道该怎么办，于是我把事情告诉了罗德里克，问他知不知老爸在打什么主意。他跟我说他会好好想一想，一会儿过后，他走入我的房间，关上了门。

罗德里克跟我说，他认为"罗利事件"让老爸很恼火，老爸打算不要我了。

我不知道要不要相信他，因为罗德里克并不是100%可靠。可罗德里克说要是我不相信，可以去检查老爸的日程记录本，自己亲眼看看就知道。于是我走进老爸的办公室，把他的日历翻到周日那一天，下面就是我的发现——

我很肯定罗德里克在作弄我，因为这些字和他的笔迹高度相似。不过老爸是个难以捉摸的人，我得等到周日那一天才能确切知道是怎么回事。

星期日

好消息是老爸今天没有卖了我，也没有送我去孤儿院。坏消息是，不担保今天过后他不会这么做。

早上10点左右，老爸叫我上车，说想带我进城。我问他进城干什么，他说"这是惊喜"。

进城的路上我们停车加油。老爸把地图和说明书随手放在汽车的仪表盘上，现在我知道我们要去的地方了——1200海岸大街。

这下我绝望了，平生第一回用了我的"甲壳虫小·姐"。

我打完电话老爸就回来了，我们进了市区。我真后悔自己看地图的时候没仔细一点，在海岸大街停车后，我才知道这是棒球馆的停车场。不过到了这个时候一切都晚了。

原来老妈给我们俩买了棒球比赛的父子票，老爸想给我一个惊喜。

警察来了，老爸花了很长时间给警察解释整件事。和警察讲清楚以后，老爸已经没有心情看棒球赛了，他直接带我回家。

我觉得有点难过，老妈给我们买的是第三排的座位，票价应该不便宜啊。

星期二

我终于弄明白昨天那个电话是怎么回事了。老爸和外婆在电话里说的是"阿甜"，不是我。

老爸老妈决定把小狗给外婆养，星期天晚上老爸把阿甜送去外婆家。老实说吧，这里没有谁真的舍不得它离开。

昨天回来之后我和老爸就没再说过话，我一直在找借口不呆在家里。昨天我找到一个挺不错的借口了。电视上有个"游戏天地"的商店广告，我的电子游戏都是在那里买的。

他们办了一个比赛，你在当地的商店打游戏，如果你胜利了就可以晋级参加全国决赛。全国赛的冠军可得一百万元的奖金。

我去的那家商店是在这周六比赛。我敢肯定无数人会来参加，我要一大早起床排队才可以排到一个好位置。

这招是我从罗德里克那里学来的。每回他想买音乐会的门票，前一天晚上他就会到街上彻夜排队。实际他也就是在那里认识了他的乐队主唱比尔。

　　罗利和他爸常常去露营，所以我知道他有帐篷。我打电话给罗利，告诉他电子游戏比赛和一百万美元奖金的事情。

　　罗利在电话里表现得很紧张。我想他还是担心我有通电的超能力之类的问题。让他冷静下来的唯一办法是我保证不会在他身上使用超能力。

　　即便我们在超能力的事情上已经说好了，罗利对彻夜排队的事还是支支吾吾。他说他爸妈不许他在这个暑假再和我见面。

　　其实我已经猜到了八八九九，不过我有一个绕开禁令的点子。我跟罗利说，我会跟我爸妈说我要去他家留宿，他可以跟他爸妈说他去柯林斯家留宿。

　　罗利还是不置可否的样子，我告诉他如果他和我一道排队，我会给他一盒橡皮熊糖果，这下他动心了。

星期六

昨晚9：00 我们在山坡上集合。罗利带了露营装备和睡袋，我带了手电筒和几根用来补充能量的巧克力棒。

我手头上没有橡皮熊糖果，不过我向罗利保证一有机会我就会买给他。

到了"游戏天地"，我发现只有我们俩，这运气好得让人难以置信。

我们在商店门口支起帐篷，这样其他人就占不了我们的地盘了。

然后我们盯着大门，确保没人插我们的队。

要稳保我们排队第一名的位子，我觉得最好的办法是轮流睡觉。我甚至主动值第一班让罗利先睡，谁叫我本就是这么好的人呢。

我值完一班，就叫醒罗利，哪知道他五秒钟不到又睡了过去。我把他摇醒，叮嘱他要保持警惕。

罗利根本就不想为自己辩解。

我本来就不喜欢电子游戏！

得靠我自己来防止别人插队了，我整夜都没有合眼。到了早上9：00我快睁不开眼睛了，我把两根巧克力棒都吃掉，好让自己坚持下去。

我的手到处沾着巧克力，我突然来了灵感。我打开帐篷的布幕，偷偷把手伸进去，装成在地上爬的蜘蛛。

我想，让罗利以为这是泥手会很好玩。帐篷里没有什么声音，我以为罗利还在睡。我正想掀开布幕看看怎么回事，手就差点被砸碎了。

我赶紧缩手，一看，我的大拇指都变紫了。

我真的被罗利气死了。不是因为他用木槌砸了我的手，而是因为他以为这样子就能阻止泥手。

　　是个傻瓜都知道你得用火或者酸才能阻止泥手，木槌只会把它惹怒的。

　　我正要好好教训罗利一顿，这时候游戏天地的人上班了，打开了前门。我尽力不去在意大拇指袭来的阵阵痛楚，精神集中在我们来这里的目的上。

　　游戏天地的人问我们干吗在商店门口搭帐篷，我说我们来这里是为了参加电子游戏竞赛。可他压根儿就不知道我说的是什么事。

　　我只好把窗上的海报扯下来给他看，让他了解最新形势。

这个职员说他们店还没有准备好举行电子游戏比赛，不过既然只有我们两个人，也许我们可以在休息室内比一场。

起初我有点恼火，不过后来我意识到要赢得这次比赛其实只要打败罗利就行了。那个职员让我们打"古怪巫师"，一局定胜负。我简直要为罗利感到难过了，因为我是古怪巫师的游戏高手。不过到比赛开始的时候，我意识到自己的大拇指已疼得不能动了，我不能按手柄的按钮。

罗利一次次瞄准我开火，我只能绕着圈圈到处跑。

罗利最后以15：0击败我。那个职员宣布罗利赢得比赛，他可以有两种选择：要么填写一堆表格参加全国决赛，要么获得一大盒葡萄干巧克力作为奖品。

不用说你也能猜到罗利选的是什么啦。

星期日

要我说，我本来应该坚持暑假呆在屋里不出门的计划，你看，从我走出屋外开始，所有麻烦事都来了。

自从罗利从我那里"盗取"了电子游戏比赛的胜利后，我再也没见过他了。自从老爸差点被我送进拘留所，他再也没跟我说过话了。

不过我觉得今天事情开始有了转机。你还记得那篇文章说"小可爱"由作者儿子接手的事么？

今天第一期漫画面世了，不过，看起来新的"小·可爱"比原版的更糟糕。

爸爸，你可以让我打的"嗝嗝"回去吗？

我拿给老爸看，他和我意见一致。

仔细瞧瞧这玩意儿！

给我看看！

这时候我意识到我们的关系已经开始解冻了。我和老爸也许不是在每件事情上都赞成对方的看法，不过至少在重要的事情上还是意见一致的。

我猜有人会说，两个人的感情建立在讨厌同一部漫画的基础上，太脆弱了，不过事实上我和老爸一起讨厌的东西非常多。

我和老爸也许不像别的两父子那么亲密，不过我觉得还好。我知道有时候过于亲密会导致什么样的后果。

今天老妈把照片都放进她的照相簿里，我意识到暑假快要过完了。我随便翻了一下，老实跟你说，我觉得照相簿完全不是这个暑假生活的准确记录。不过我想还是拍照片的人说了算吧。

"这就是我想要的蛋糕！"

赫夫利家三代男士聚餐。

罗德里克说："谁还用得着去海滩？"

一个魔术般神奇的独立日。

噼里，啪啦！格雷在泳池里玩得欢。

噢！妈妈被拍到了。

格雷觉得和救生员大哥哥在一起很"酷"。

最铁的哥们！

TO JONATHAN

DIARY
of a
Wimpy Kid

⑧

by Jeff Kinney

Saturday

Mom was acting extra-cheery this morning, and I could tell she had something up her sleeve.

At 10:00 she said we all needed to get in the station wagon, and when I asked her where we were going, she said it was a "surprise".

I noticed Mom had packed sunscreen and bathing suits and stuff in the back of the station wagon, so I thought we must be headed for the beach.

But when I asked her if I was right, Mom said the place we were going was BETTER than the beach.

Wherever we were going, it was taking a long time to get there. And it wasn't that fun being stuck in the backseat with Rodrick and Manny.

Manny was sitting in between me and Rodrick on the hump. At one point Rodrick decided to tell Manny the hump was the worst seat in the car because it was the smallest and least comfortable.

Well, that totally set Manny off.

Eventually, Mom and Dad got sick of Manny's crying. Mom said I had to take a turn on the hump because I'm the second youngest and it was "only fair". So every time Dad ran over a pothole, my head hit the roof of the car.

At about 2:00 I was getting really hungry, so I asked if we could stop for some fast food. Dad wouldn't pull over, because he said the people at fast-food restaurants are "idiots".

Well, I know why he thinks that. Every time Dad goes to the fried chicken place over near our house, he tries to place his order through the trash can.

I saw a sign for a pizza place, and I begged Mom and Dad to let us eat there. But I guess Mom was trying to save money, because she came prepared.

A half hour later we pulled into a big parking lot, and I knew exactly where we were.

We were at the Slipslide Water Park, where we used to go as kids. And I mean LITTLE kids. It's really a place meant for people at Manny's age.

Mom must've heard me and Rodrick groan in the backseat. She said we were gonna have a great day as a family and it would be the highlight of our summer vacation.

I have bad memories of the Slipslide Water Park. One time Grandpa took me there, and he left me in the waterslide area for practically the whole day. He said he was gonna go read his book and he'd meet me there in three hours. But I didn't actually go on any slides because of the sign at the entrance.

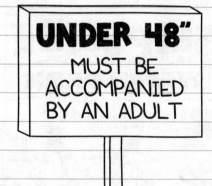

I thought you had to be forty-eight years old to ride, but it turns out the two little lines next to the number meant "inches".

So I basically wasted my day waiting for Grandpa to come back and get me, and then we had to leave.

Rodrick has bad memories of the Slipslide Water Park, too. Last year his band got booked to do a show on the music stage they have near the wave pool. Rodrick's band asked the park people to set them up with a smoke machine so they could have some special effects for their show.

But somebody screwed up, and they set Rodrick's band up with a BUBBLE machine instead.

I found out the reason Mom took us to the water park today: It was half-price for families. Unfortunately, it looked like just about every family in the state was there, too.

When we got through the gates, Mom rented a stroller for Manny. I convinced her to spend a little more money and rent a double stroller, because I knew it was gonna be a long day and I wanted to conserve my energy.

Mom parked the stroller near the wave pool, which was so crowded you could barely even see the water. After we put on our sunscreen and found a place to sit, I felt a few raindrops, and then I heard thunder. Then an announcement came over the loudspeaker.

DUE TO LIGHTNING, THE SLIPSLIDE WATER PARK IS NOW CLOSED. THANK YOU FOR COMING, AND HAVE A NICE DAY.

Everyone hit the exits and got in their cars. But with all the people trying to leave at the exact same time, it was a total traffic jam.

Manny tried to entertain everyone by telling jokes.

At first Mom and Dad were encouraging him. But after a while, Manny's jokes didn't even make sense.

We were low on gas, so we had to turn off the air conditioner and wait for the parking lot to clear up.

Mom said she had a headache, and she went to the back to lie down. An hour later traffic finally thinned out, and we got onto the highway.

We stopped for gas, and about forty-five minutes later we were home. Dad told me to wake Mom up, but when I looked in the back of the station wagon, Mom wasn't there.

For a few minutes nobody knew where she went. Then we realized the only place she could be was at the gas station. She must've gotten out to use the bathroom when we stopped, and nobody noticed.

Sure enough, that's where she was. We were glad to see her, but I don't think she was too happy to see US.

Mom didn't really say anything on the ride back.
Something tells me she's had her fill of family
togetherness for a while, and that's good,
because I have, too.

Sunday
I really wish we didn't go on that trip yesterday,
because if we stayed home, my fish would still be alive.

Before we left for our trip I fed my fish, and Mom
said I should feed Rodrick's fish, too. Rodrick's fish
was in a bowl on top of the refrigerator, and I'm
pretty sure Rodrick hadn't fed his fish or cleaned
the bowl once.

I think Rodrick's fish was living off of the algae growing on the glass.

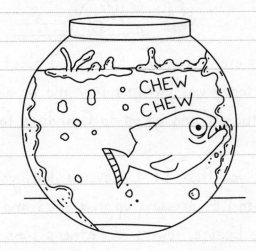

When Mom saw Rodrick's bowl, she thought it was disgusting. So she took his fish and put it in my bowl.

When we got home from the water park, I went straight to the kitchen to feed my fish. But he was gone, and it wasn't a big mystery what happened to him.

I didn't even have time to feel sad about it, because today was Father's Day and we all had to get in the car and go up to Grandpa's for brunch.

I'll tell you this: If I'm ever a dad, you're not gonna see ME dressing up in a shirt and tie and going to Leisure Towers on Father's Day. I'm gonna go off by myself and have some FUN. But Mom said she thought it would be good for the three generations of Heffley men to be together.

I guess I must've been picking at my food, because Dad asked me what was wrong. I told him I was bummed out because my fish died. Dad said he didn't really know what to say because he'd never had a pet die before.

He said he used to have a dog named Nutty when he was a kid, but Nutty ran away to a butterfly farm.

I've heard Dad tell this same story about Nutty and the butterfly farm a million times, but I didn't wanna be rude and cut him off.

Then Grandpa spoke up and said he had a "confession" to make. He said that Nutty didn't actually run away to a butterfly farm. Grandpa said what REALLY happened was that he accidentally ran over the dog when he was backing his car out of the driveway.

WAS THAT FRANK'S SKATEBOARD?

Grandpa said he made up the butterfly farm story so he didn't have to tell Dad the truth, but that now they could have a good laugh over it.

But Dad was MAD. He told us to get in the car, and he left Grandpa with the bill for brunch. Dad didn't say anything on the way home. He just dropped us off at the house and drove away.

SCREECH

Dad was gone for a long time, and I was starting to think maybe he was gonna just take the rest of the day for himself. But he showed up an hour later carrying a big cardboard box.

Dad put the box on the floor, and believe it or not, there was a DOG in there.

Mom didn't seem too thrilled that Dad went out and bought a dog without checking with her first. I don't think Dad has ever even bought a pair of pants for himself without getting Mom's OK beforehand. But I think she could see that Dad was happy, so she let him keep it.

At dinner, Mom said we should come up with a name for the dog.

I wanted to name it something cool like Shredder or Ripjaw, but Mom said my ideas were too "violent".

Manny's ideas were a whole lot worse, though. He wanted to name the dog an animal name like Elephant or Zebra.

Rodrick liked the animal name idea, and he said we should call the dog Turtle.

Mom said we should call the dog Sweetheart. I thought that was a really terrible idea, because the dog is a BOY, not a girl.

But before any of us could fight it, Dad agreed
with Mom's idea.

I think Dad was willing to go with anything Mom
came up with if it meant he didn't have to take
the dog back. But something tells me Uncle Joe
would not approve of our dog's name.

Dad told Rodrick he should go to the mall to buy
a bowl and get the dog's name printed on it, and
here's what Rodrick came back with —

I guess that's what you get when you send the worst speller in the family off to do your errands.

Wednesday
I was really happy when we got our dog at first, but now I'm starting to have second thoughts.

The dog's actually been driving me crazy. A few nights ago a commercial came on TV, and it showed some gophers popping in and out of their holes. Sweetie seemed pretty interested in that, so Dad said —

WHERE ARE THE GOPHERS, SWEETIE? WHERE ARE THEY, BOY?

That got Sweetie all riled up, and he started barking at the TV.

Now Sweetie barks at the TV CONSTANTLY, and the only thing that gets him to stop is when the commercial with the gophers comes back on.

But what really bugs me about the dog is that he likes to sleep in my bed, and I'm afraid he'll bite my hand off if I try to move him.

And he doesn't just sleep in my bed. He sleeps right smack in the middle.

Dad comes in my room at 7:00 every morning to take Sweetie out. But I guess me and the dog have something in common, because he doesn't like getting out of bed in the morning, either. So Dad turns the lights on and off to try to make the dog wake up.

Yesterday Dad couldn't get Sweetie to go outside, so he tried something new. He went to the front of the house and rang the doorbell, which made the dog shoot out of bed like a rocket.

The only problem was, he used my face as a launching pad.

It must've been raining outside this morning, because when Sweetie came back in he was shivering and soaking wet. Then he tried to get under the covers with me to get warm. Luckily, the muddy hand has given me a lot of practice with this sort of thing, so I was able to keep him out.

Thursday

This morning Dad wasn't able to get the dog out of my bed no matter WHAT he tried. So he went to work, and about an hour later Sweetie woke me up to take him outside. I wrapped myself in my blanket and then let the dog out the front door and waited for him to do his business. But Sweetie decided to make a run for it, and I had to chase after him.

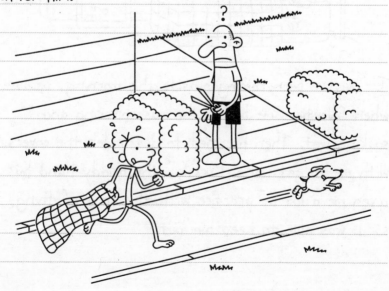

You know, I was actually having a pretty decent summer until Sweetie came along. He's ruining the two things that are the most important to me: television and sleep.

And you know how Dad is always getting on my case about lying around all day? Well, Sweetie is twice as bad as me, but Dad's CRAZY about that dog.

I don't think the feeling is mutual, though. Dad is always trying to get the dog to give him a kiss on the nose, but Sweetie won't do it.

I can kind of understand why the dog doesn't like Dad.

The only person Sweetie really likes is Mom, even though she barely pays him any attention. And I can tell that's starting to drive Dad a little nuts.

I think Sweetie is just more of a ladies' man. So I guess that's something else we have in common.

JULY

<u>Saturday</u>

Last night I was working on a new comic to replace "Li'l Cutie." I figured there would be a lot of competition for the open slot, so I wanted to come up with something that really stood out. I made up this comic called "Hey, People!" that's sort of like a half cartoon, half advice column. I figure I can use it to make the world a better place, or at least a better place for ME.

UM...LET'S SEE...I GUESS... HMM...

WHEN ORDERING FROM A FAST-FOOD RESTAURANT, TRY TO DECIDE WHAT YOU WANT <u>BEFORE</u> YOU GET TO THE FRONT OF THE LINE.

I figured since Dad reads the comics, I might as well write a few that were specifically targeted at him.

I would've written a bunch of comics last night, but Sweetie was driving me crazy and I couldn't concentrate.

While I was drawing, the dog was sitting on my pillow licking his paws and his tail, and he was really getting into it.

Whenever Sweetie does that, I have to remember to flip the pillow over when I go to bed. Last night I forgot, and when I lay down I put my head right on the wet spot.

Speaking of licking, Sweetie finally kissed Dad last night. It's probably because Dad had potato chips on his breath, and I think dogs have an automatic response to that sort of thing.

I didn't have the heart to tell Dad that Sweetie had just spent the past half hour on my pillow licking his rear end.

Anyway, I'm hoping I can write a few more comics tonight, because I'm not gonna be able to get any work done tomorrow. Tomorrow's the Fourth of July, and Mom is making the whole family go to the town pool.

I tried to get out of it, mostly because I want to make it through the summer without having to walk past the shower guys. But I think Mom's still hoping to have one perfect family day this summer, so there's no use fighting it.

Monday

My Fourth of July started out pretty rough. When I got to the pool, I tried to get through the locker room as quickly as I could. But the shower guys were really chatty, and they didn't make it easy on me.

Then Mom told me she left her sunglasses out in the car, so I had to go BACK through the shower area to the parking lot. I wore Mom's sunglasses on the return trip to make it clear I wasn't interested in conversation, but that didn't work out so good, either.

Seriously, I wish those guys would just take a shower at home before they came to the pool. Because once you see somebody like that, you can never look at them the same way again.

After I got past the locker room, things didn't get a whole lot better. The scene was just about how I remembered it, except more crowded. I guess everyone had the same idea to spend the Fourth at the pool.

The only time the pool cleared out was when the lifeguard called a fifteen-minute rest break and all the kids had to get out of the water.

I think the idea behind rest breaks is to give adults a little time to enjoy the pool, but I don't know how they're supposed to relax with three hundred kids waiting for the break to be over.

When I was younger I used to just go swim in the baby pool during the fifteen-minute rest break, but that was before I knew what went on in there.

MAMA, I'M PEEING!

The only area of the pool that wasn't a complete madhouse was the deep end, and that's where the diving boards are. I haven't been in the deep end since I was eight years old, when Rodrick talked me into jumping off the high dive.

Rodrick was always trying to get me to jump off the high dive, but that tall ladder really scared me. He told me I needed to conquer my fears or I'd never become a man.

Then one day Rodrick told me that there was a clown at the top of the diving board who was handing out free toys, and that got my attention.

But by the time I realized Rodrick was full of baloney, it was too late.

Anyway, today Mom got everyone together to go to the picnic area because they were giving out free watermelon.

But I've got a fear of watermelon, too. Rodrick is always telling me that if you eat the seeds, then a watermelon will grow in your stomach.

I don't know if he's telling the truth or not, but school's only a couple of months away, so I'm not willing to take the risk.

When it started getting dark, everyone put their blankets out on the lawn to watch the fireworks display. We sat staring up at the sky for a long time, but nothing was happening.

Then someone came on the loudspeaker and said that the show was canceled because someone left the fireworks out in the rain last night and they got soaked. Some little kids started to cry, so a couple of grown-ups tried to create their own fireworks show.

Luckily, the fireworks display at the country club down the road started right about then. It was a little hard to see over the trees, but at that point I don't think anyone really cared.

Tuesday

This morning I was sitting at the kitchen table flipping through the comics, and I came across something that almost made me spit out my cereal.

It was a two-page back-to-school ad, right where any kid could see it.

I can't believe it's actually LEGAL to run a back-to-school ad two months before school starts. Anyone who would do that kind of thing must really not like kids.

I'm sure back-to-school ads are gonna start popping up all over the place now, and the next thing you know, Mom is gonna be telling me it's time to go clothes shopping. And with Mom, that's an all-day affair.

So I asked Mom if Dad could take me clothes shopping instead, and she said yes. I think she saw it as some kind of father-son bonding opportunity.

But I told Dad he could just go without me and pick out whatever he wanted.

Well, THAT was a dumb move, because Dad did
all of his shopping at the pharmacy.

Before I saw that ad, my day was bad enough
already. It rained again this morning, so Sweetie
tried to get under the covers with me after Dad
took him out.

I guess I must've been a little off my game,
because the dog found a gap between the blanket
and the bed and managed to get through.

And let me tell you, there's nothing more terrifying
than being trapped under your covers wearing nothing
but underwear with a wet dog crawling all over you.

I was stewing about the dog and that back-to-school ad when my whole day turned around. Mom had printed out some pictures from the Fourth, and she left them lying on the kitchen table.

In one of the pictures you could see a lifeguard in the background. It was a little hard to tell, but I'm pretty sure the lifeguard was Heather Hills.

It was so crowded at the pool yesterday that I
didn't even notice the lifeguards. And if that really
WAS Heather Hills, I can't believe I missed her.

Heather Hills is the sister of Holly Hills, who is one
of the cutest girls in my class. But Heather's in
HIGH school, which is a whole different league
than middle school.

This Heather Hills thing is changing my whole
perspective on the town pool. In fact, I'm
starting to rethink my whole SUMMER. The dog
has ruined all the fun of being at home, and I
realized that if I don't do something quick, I
won't have anything good to say about my vacation.

So starting tomorrow I'm gonna have a whole new attitude. And hopefully by the time I get back to school, I'll have a high school girlfriend, too.

Wednesday

Mom was really happy I was willing to go to the pool with her and Manny today, and she said she was proud I was finally putting my family in front of video games. I didn't mention Heather Hills to Mom, because I don't need her getting in the middle of my love life.

When we got there, I wanted to go straight to the pool area and see if Heather was on duty. But then I realized I'd better be prepared in case she was.

So I made a pit stop in the bathroom and lathered myself in suntan oil. Then I did a bunch of push-ups and sit-ups to really make my muscles pop.

I was probably in there for about fifteen minutes. I was checking myself out in the mirror when I heard someone in a stall clear his throat.

Well, that was pretty embarrassing, because it meant whoever was in there could see me flexing in front of the mirror the whole time. And if that person was anything like ME, he couldn't go to the bathroom until he had complete privacy.

I figured the person in the stall couldn't see my face, so at least he didn't know who I was. I was just about to slip out of the bathroom when I heard Mom at the front of the locker room.

Mom wanted to know what took me so long and why I looked so "shiny," but I was already looking past her and scanning the lifeguard stands to see if Heather Hills was on deck.

130

And sure enough, she was. I went right over to her and parked myself underneath her chair.

Every once in a while I'd say something witty, and I think I was definitely impressing her.

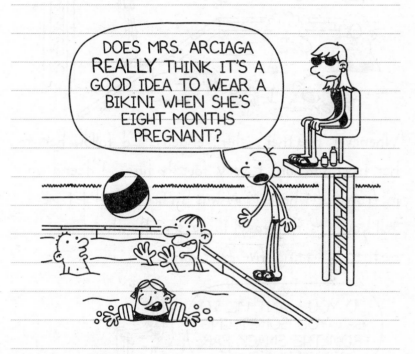

I'd get Heather a new cup of water whenever it looked like she needed a refill, and every time some kid would do something wrong, I'd speak up so Heather didn't have to.

Whenever Heather's shift ended, I'd follow her to her next station. Every fourth time, I'd end up in front of where Mom was sitting. And let me tell you, it's not easy to be smooth when your mother is sitting five feet away.

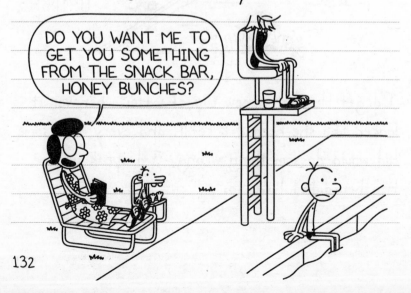

I just hope Heather knows that I would do
ANYTHING for her. If she wants someone to
put suntan lotion on her back or towel her off
after she takes a dip in the pool, I'm the man
for the job.

I basically hung out with Heather until it was
time to go. On my way home I was thinking
that if the rest of my vacation goes like today,
this WILL be the best summer ever, just like
Mom predicted. In fact, the only thing that
can ruin things now is that stupid muddy hand.
I'm sure it'll show up at the exact wrong moment
and spoil everything.

Wednesday

I've been hanging out with Heather every single day for the past week.

I realized my friends at school will never believe it when I tell them about me and Heather, so I asked Mom to take a picture of me standing next to the lifeguard chair.

Mom didn't have her camera, so she had to use her cell phone. But she couldn't figure out how to take a picture with it, and I ended up standing there for a long time looking like a fool.

PRESS...THE LITTLE... GREEN... BUTTON!

?

I finally got Mom to press the right button to take a picture, but when she did, the camera was pointed the wrong way and she took a picture of herself. See, this is why I always say that technology is wasted on grown-ups.

I got Mom to point the camera at me, but right at that moment her phone rang and she answered it.

Mom talked for about five minutes, and by the time she was done, Heather was on to her next shift. But that didn't stop Mom from taking the picture anyway.

Friday

Relying on Mom for my ride to the pool is starting to become a problem. Mom doesn't want to go to the pool every day, and when she DOES go, she only stays a few hours.

I like to be at the pool from the time it opens until the time it closes so I can maximize my time with Heather. I wasn't about to ask Rodrick to drive me to the pool in his van because he always makes me sit in the back, and there are no seats.

I realized I need my OWN transportation, and luckily I found a solution yesterday.

One of our neighbors left a bike out by the curb, and I took it before anyone else could.

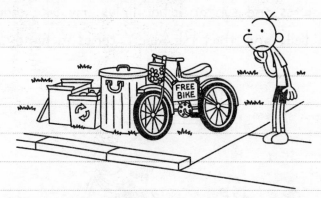

I rode the bike home and parked it in the garage. When Dad saw it, he said it was a "girl bike" and I should get rid of it.

But I'll tell you at least two reasons a girl bike is better than a boy bike. Number one, girl bikes have big, cushiony seats, and that's really important when you're riding in your bathing suit.

GIRL SEAT

BOY SEAT

And number two, girl bikes have those baskets on
the handlebars, which are good for carrying your
video games and suntan lotion. Plus, my bike came
with a bell, and that REALLY comes in handy.

Monday
I guess I should've known that a bike that
was left out with the trash wasn't gonna last
very long.

I was riding home from the pool yesterday, and
the bike started getting all wobbly. Then the
front wheel popped right off. So today I had
to ask Mom for a ride to the pool.

When we got there, Mom said I had to take
Manny with me through the locker room. She said
he's getting too old to go through the women's
locker room with her, so I guess they must have
the same shower situation in there as they do in
the men's locker room.

It should've taken about five seconds to get
Manny from one end of the locker room to the
other, but it took about ten minutes instead.

Manny goes everywhere with Mom, so he had
never actually BEEN in a men's bathroom before.
He was really curious and wanted to check everything
out. At one point I had to stop him from washing
his hands in the urinal because I guess he thought
it was a sink.

I didn't want Manny to have to walk through the shower area and see the things I've seen. So I got a towel out of my bag and was gonna put it over Manny's eyes when we walked past the shower guys. But in the two seconds it took me to get my towel, Manny was gone. And you'll never believe where he went.

I knew I had to rescue Manny, so I closed my eyes as tight as I could and went in to save him.

I was really nervous about touching one of the
shower guys, and for a second there I thought
I did.

I had to open my eyes to find Manny, and then I
grabbed him and got out as fast as I could.

When we got to the other side, Manny seemed
fine, but I don't think I'll ever totally recover
from that experience.

I kind of staggered over to my spot underneath
Heather's lifeguard chair. Then I started taking
deep breaths to calm myself down.

Five minutes later some kid who must've eaten too
much ice cream threw up behind Heather's chair.
Heather looked behind her, and then she looked
down like she was waiting for me to do something.
I guess the noble thing to do was to clean up the
mess for Heather, but this was really beyond the
call of duty.

Anyway, I've been doing a lot of thinking lately, and
I've realized that I need to let this summer romance
cool off a little.

Plus, Heather's going off to college next year, and those long-distance relationships never really seem to work out.

AUGUST

Tuesday

We ran into the Jeffersons at the supermarket today. Me and Rowley haven't spoken to each other in over a month, so it was kind of awkward.

Mrs. Jefferson said they were buying groceries for their trip to the beach next week. That kind of irritated me because that's where MY family was supposed to go this summer. But then Mrs. Jefferson said something that really threw me for a loop.

HOW WOULD GREGORY LIKE TO **JOIN** US?

Mr. Jefferson didn't look too thrilled with that idea, but before he could speak up Mom chimed in.

WHY, GREGORY WOULD LOVE TO!

Something about the whole incident seemed a little fishy to me. I'm kind of wondering if it was a setup, with Mom and Mrs. Jefferson conspiring to get me and Rowley back together.

Believe me, Rowley's the LAST person I want to spend a week with. But then I realized if I went to the beach with the Jeffersons, I'd get to ride the Cranium Shaker. So maybe my summer won't be such a bust after all.

Monday
I knew I made a mistake coming on this beach trip when I saw where we were staying.

QUIET
COVE

My family always rents a condo in the high-rises right near the boardwalk, but the place where the Jeffersons are staying is a log cabin about five miles from the beach. We went inside the cabin, and there was no TV or computer or ANYTHING with a screen on it.

I asked what we were supposed to do for entertainment, and Mrs. Jefferson said —

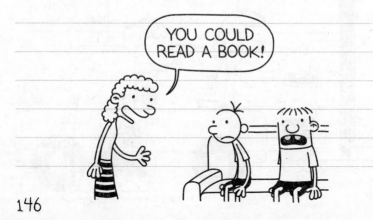

YOU COULD READ A BOOK!

I thought that was a good one, and I was about to tell Rowley his mom was pretty funny. But she came back a second later with a bunch of reading material.

So that just CONFIRMED Mom was in on this plan from the beginning.

All three Jeffersons read their books right up until it was time to eat. Dinner was OK, but dessert was awful. Mrs. Jefferson is one of those moms who sneaks healthy food into your snacks, and her brownies were full of spinach.

I don't think it's a good idea to grind up vegetables and put them in kids' desserts, because then they don't know what the real thing is supposed to taste like.

The first time Rowley had a regular brownie was at my house, and believe me, it wasn't pretty.

After dinner Mrs. Jefferson called us all into the living room to play games. I was hoping we were gonna play something normal like cards, but the Jeffersons have their own idea of fun.

The Jeffersons played a game called "I Love You Because," and when it was my turn, I passed.

Then we played charades, and when it was Rowley's turn, he was a dog.

At about 9:00 Mr. Jefferson told us it was time for bed. That's when I found out the sleeping situation at the Jeffersons' cabin was worse than the entertainment situation.

There was only one bed, so I told Rowley we could make a deal: We'd flip a coin, and one guy would get the bed and the other would sleep on the floor.

But Rowley took a look at the crusty shag carpet and decided he didn't want to risk it. I decided I wasn't willing to sleep on the floor, either. So I got into bed with Rowley and just stayed as far away from him as possible.

Rowley started snoring right away, but I was having trouble falling asleep with half my body hanging off the bed. I was finally starting to drift off when Rowley let out a scream like he was being attacked.

150

For a second there I thought the muddy hand had finally caught up with us.

Rowley's parents came running in to see what happened.

Rowley said he had a nightmare that there was a chicken hiding underneath him.

So Rowley's parents spent the next twenty minutes trying to calm him down and telling him it was just a bad dream and there really was no chicken.

Nobody bothered to check on how I was doing after falling off the bed onto my face.

Rowley spent the rest of the night sleeping in his parents' room, which was fine with me. Because without Rowley and his chicken dreams to keep me awake, I was able to get a good night's sleep.

Wednesday
I've been stuck inside this cabin for three days now, and I'm really starting to lose my mind.

I've been trying to get Mr. and Mrs. Jefferson to take us to the boardwalk, but they say it's too "noisy" there.

I've never gone this long without TV or computers or video games, and I'm starting to feel kind of desperate. When Mr. Jefferson works late at night on his laptop, I sneak downstairs and watch him just to get a glimpse of the outside world.

I've tried to get Mr. Jefferson to let me use his laptop a couple of times, but he says it's his "work computer" and he doesn't want me to mess anything up. Last night I was at my breaking point, so I did something a little risky.

When Mr. Jefferson got up to use the bathroom,
I jumped at my chance.

I rattled off an e-mail to Mom as quick as I
could, then ran upstairs and got into bed.

TO: Heffley, Susan
SUBJECT: SOS

HELP HELP GET ME OUT OF HERE THESE
PEOPLE ARE DRIVING ME CRAZY

When I came downstairs for breakfast this morning,
Mr. Jefferson didn't look too happy to see me.

It turns out that I sent that e-mail from Mr. Jefferson's work account, and Mom answered back.

TO: Jefferson, Robert
SUBJECT: RE: SOS
_____

Family vacations can be a challenge!
Is Gregory not behaving himself?

- Susan

I thought Mr. Jefferson was gonna really let me have it, but he didn't say anything at all. Then Mrs. Jefferson said maybe we could go to the boardwalk later on this afternoon and spend an hour or two there.

Well, that's all I was ever asking for. A few hours is all I really need.

If I can just ride the Cranium Shaker once, I'll feel like this trip wasn't a total waste of time.

Friday

I'm back home from the beach two days early, and if you wanna know the reason why, it's kind of a long story.

The Jeffersons took me and Rowley to the boardwalk yesterday afternoon. I wanted to go on the Cranium Shaker right away, but the line was too long, so we decided to get some food and come back later.

We got some ice cream, but Mrs. Jefferson only ordered one cone for the four of us to share.

Mom gave me thirty dollars to spend at the beach, and I blew twenty of it on this one carnival game.

I was trying to win a giant stuffed caterpillar, but I think they have those games rigged so you can't succeed.

Rowley watched me blow my twenty dollars, and then he asked his dad to buy him the EXACT same giant caterpillar at a shop next door. And the thing that really stinks is that it only cost him ten bucks.

I think Mr. Jefferson is making a big mistake with a move like that. Now Rowley feels like a winner even though he isn't.

I've had my own experience with that sort of thing. Last year when I was on the swim team, they had this special swim meet I got invited to on a Sunday.

When I showed up, I realized none of the GOOD swimmers were there. It was only the kids who had never won a ribbon before.

At first I was pretty happy, because I thought I might actually WIN something for once.

I still didn't do well, though. My event was the 100-meter freestyle, and I got so pooped that I had to WALK the last lap.

But the judges didn't disqualify me. And at the end of the night, I got a first-place ribbon, which my parents handed to me.

In fact, EVERYONE walked away with first-place ribbons, even Tommy Lam, who got turned around in the backstroke and swam the wrong way.

When I got home, I was confused. But then Rodrick saw me with my first-place Champions ribbon, and he gave me the scoop.

Rodrick told me the Champions meet is just a scam put on by parents to make their kids feel like winners.

I guess parents think they're doing their kids a favor by going through with all that, but if you ask me, I think it just causes more problems down the road.

I remember when I used to be on the tee-ball team and everyone would cheer even when I struck out. Then the next year, in junior baseball, all my teammates and the other parents would boo me off the field if I dropped a pop fly or something.

All I'm saying is, if Rowley's parents wanna make him feel good about himself, they can't do it now when he's a kid and then walk away. They've gotta stick with him all the way through.

After the caterpillar thing we just walked up and down the boardwalk, waiting for the line for the Cranium Shaker to go down. Then I saw something that got my attention.

It was that girl from Rodrick's keychain picture. But here's the thing: She wasn't a real person. She was a CARDBOARD CUTOUT.

SOUVENIR
KEYCHAIN
PHOTOS
$5

I felt like an idiot for ever thinking that she was a real girl. Then I realized I could buy my OWN keychain picture and impress all the guys at school. I might even be able to make some money by charging them to look at it.

I paid my five bucks and posed for my photo. Unfortunately, the Jeffersons got into the picture WITH me, so now my souvenir keychain is pretty much worthless.

I was really mad, but I forgot all about it when I saw that the line for the Cranium Shaker was down to a few people. I ran over to the ride and used my last five dollars to pay for a ticket.

I thought Rowley was right behind me, but he was hanging back about ten feet. I guess he was too scared to go on.

I was starting to have second thoughts myself, but it was too late. After the ride operator strapped me in, he locked the cage and I knew there was no turning back.

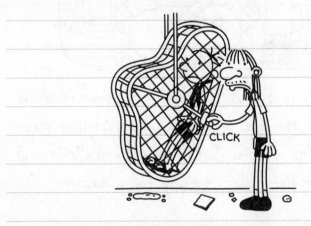

CLICK

Well, I wish I had spent more time watching what the Cranium Shaker actually DID to a person, because I never would've gotten on if I had.

It flips you upside down about a million times and then throws you toward the ground so your face is about six inches from the pavement. Then it sends you spinning backward up to the sky again.

And the whole time the cage you're in is creaking, and all the bolts look like they're about to come loose. I tried to get someone to stop the ride, but nobody could hear me over the pounding heavy metal music.

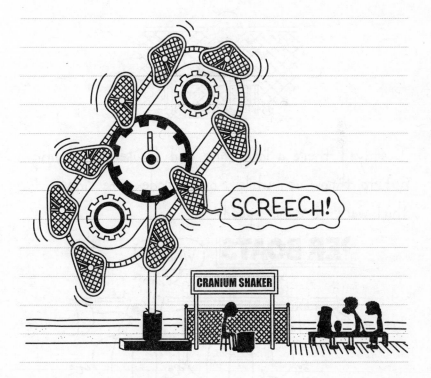

SCREECH!

CRANIUM SHAKER

It was the most nauseous I've ever felt in my life. And when I say that, I mean even more than after I had to get Manny out of the shower area at the town pool. If this is what it takes to be a "man," I am definitely not ready yet.

When the ride finally ended, I could barely walk. So I sat down on a bench and waited for the boardwalk to stop spinning.

I stayed there a long time and focused on trying not to throw up, while Rowley rode some rides that were more his speed.

After Rowley was done with his kiddie rides, his
dad bought him a boppy balloon and a shirt from
the souvenir shop.

A half hour later I was finally ready to try
standing up and walking around again. But when
I got on my feet, Mr. Jefferson said it was
time to go.

I asked him if we could just play a few games in
the arcade, and he said OK even though he didn't
seem happy about it.

I had spent all the money Mom gave me, so I told
Mr. Jefferson twenty dollars would probably do it.
But all he was willing to offer me was a dollar.

I think the arcade was too loud for Mr. and Mrs. Jefferson, so they didn't want to go inside. They told us to go in by ourselves and meet them outside in ten minutes.

I went to the back of the arcade, where they have this game called Thunder Volt. I spent about fifty dollars on that game last year, and I got the high score. I wanted Rowley to see my name at the top of the list, because I wanted to show him what it was like to win something without it being handed to you.

Well, my name was still at the top of the list, but the person who got the NEXT highest score must've been jealous they couldn't beat me.

```
 HIGH SCORES
 1. GREG HEFFLEY............... 25320
 2. IS AN IDIOT ..................... 25310
 3. JARHEAD 71 ................... 24200
 4. RECKLESS ..................... 22100
 5. CRAVEN1..................... 21500
 6. POKECHIMP88.............. 21250
 7. WILD DOG.................... 21200
 8. ZIPPY.......................... 20300
 9. SNARL CARL................. 20100
10. LEIGHANDREW .............. 19250
```

I unplugged the machine to try and wipe out the high scores, but they were burned into the screen permanently.

I was gonna just spend our money on some other game, but then I remembered a trick Rodrick told me about, and I realized we could make the dollar last a lot longer.

Me and Rowley walked outside and went underneath
the boardwalk. Then I slipped the dollar bill up
between the planks of wood and waited for our
first victim.

Eventually, a teenager spotted the dollar sticking
out of the boardwalk.

When he went to grab it, I pulled the dollar bill
through the slat at the last second.

I have to hand it to Rodrick, because this was
actually a lot of fun.

The teenagers we pranked weren't too happy,
though, and they came after us. Me and Rowley
ran as fast as we could, and we didn't stop until
we were pretty sure we shook those guys.

But I STILL didn't feel safe. I asked Rowley to
show me some of the moves he learned in karate so
we could handle those guys if they found us.

But Rowley said he's a gold belt in karate and he wasn't going to teach his moves to a "no belt."

We hid there a while more, but the teenagers never showed up, and eventually we decided the coast was clear. That's when we realized we were underneath Kiddie Land, so there was a whole new batch of victims for our dollar bill trick right above our heads. And we got a MUCH better reaction out of those kids than we did from the teenagers.

ZIP

But one of the kids was really fast, and he grabbed the dollar before I could pull it down. So me and Rowley had to go up on the boardwalk to get it back.

This kid wasn't budging, though. I tried to explain the concept of personal property to him, but he STILL wouldn't give us our money.

I was getting pretty frustrated with this kid, and that's when Rowley's parents showed up. I was pretty glad to see them because I figured if ANYONE could talk some sense into this kid, it was Mr. Jefferson.

But Mr. Jefferson was mad, and I mean REALLY mad. He said he and Mrs. Jefferson had been looking all over for us for the past hour and they were ready to call the police to report us missing.

Then he told us we had to get in the car. But on the way to the parking lot, we walked past the arcade. I asked Mr. Jefferson if we could please have another dollar since we never did get to spend that one he gave us.

But I guess that wasn't the right thing to ask, because he took us back to the car without saying a word.

When we got back to the cabin, Mr. Jefferson said me and Rowley had to go straight to our room. That really stunk, because it wasn't even 8:00 and it was still light outside.

But Mr. Jefferson said we had to go to bed and that he didn't want to hear a peep out of us until morning. Rowley was taking it really hard. From the way he was acting, I don't think he's ever been in trouble with his dad before.

I decided to lighten the mood a little bit. I walked around on the shag carpet and then gave Rowley a static electricity shock as a joke.

That seemed to get Rowley to snap out of it.
He walked around in a circle for about five minutes
rubbing his feet on the carpet, and then got me
back while I was brushing my teeth.

I couldn't let Rowley one-up me like that, so
when he got into bed I got his boppy balloon,
pulled back the giant rubber band, and let it rip.

176

If I had to do it again, maybe I wouldn't have pulled back so hard.

When Rowley saw the red mark on his arm he screamed, and I knew that was gonna attract attention. Sure enough, his parents were up in our room in five seconds.

I tried to explain that the mark on Rowley's arm was from a rubber band, but that didn't seem to matter to the Jeffersons.

They called my parents, and two hours later Dad was at the cabin to pick me up and take me home.

Monday
Dad's really mad that he had to drive four hours round-trip to come get me. But Mom wasn't mad at all. She said the incident between me and Rowley was just "horseplay" and she was glad we were "pals" again.

But Dad is still mad, and it's been really chilly between us ever since we got back. Mom's been trying to get the two of us to do something like go to the movies together so we can "make peace," but I think right now it's best for me and Dad to just stay out of each other's way.

I think Dad's bad mood is here to stay, though, and part of it has nothing to do with me. When I opened up today's paper, here's what I saw in the Arts section —

Arts

Beloved comic to continue

Tyler Post will pen new "Li'l Cutie" comics, the first of which will appear in the paper a week from Sunday.

"Li'l Cutie" to be carried on by original cartoonist's son

In a stunning development, Tyler Post, the son of "Li'l Cutie" cartoonist Bob Post, will take up the pen and carry on his father's enduring one-panel comic.

"I didn't really have a job or any big plans, so one day I said, 'How hard can it be?' " said Tyler, who, at 32, is living with his father. It is widely believed that the Li'l Cutie character is based
See **CUTIE**, page A2

Related: Leisure Towers residents rejoice, page A3

Last night Dad came into my room and talked to me, which was the first time we spoke to each other in about three days. He said he wanted to make sure I was around on Sunday, and I said I would be.

Later on I heard him talking to someone on the phone, and he seemed to be acting kind of secretive.

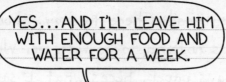

YES...AND I'LL LEAVE HIM WITH ENOUGH FOOD AND WATER FOR A WEEK.

After that I asked Dad if he was taking me anywhere in particular on Sunday, and that seemed to make him really uncomfortable. He said no, but he wouldn't look me in the eye.

Now I knew Dad wasn't telling the truth, so I started to get kind of worried. Dad was willing to ship me off to a military academy before, and I wouldn't put anything past him.

I didn't know what to do, so I told Rodrick what was going on and asked him if he had any theories about what Dad was up to. He told me he'd think about it, and a little while later he came up to my room and shut the door.

Rodrick told me he thought Dad was so mad about the Rowley thing that he was gonna get rid of me.

I wasn't sure if I believed him, because Rodrick's not always 100% reliable. But Rodrick told me if I didn't believe him I should go check out Dad's day planner and see for myself. So I went into Dad's office and opened his calendar to Sunday, and here's what I found —

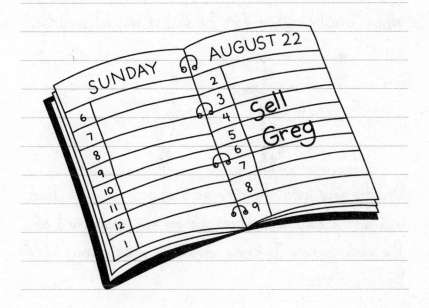

I'm pretty sure Rodrick was pulling my leg,
because it looked an awful lot like his handwriting.
But Dad's kind of an unpredictable guy, so I
guess I'll just have to wait until Sunday to know
for sure.

Sunday
The good news is Dad didn't sell me or give me
away to an orphanage today. The bad news is,
after what happened, he probably will.

At about 10:00 this morning, Dad said to get in
the car because he wanted to take me into the city.
When I asked what for, he said it was a "surprise."

On the way into the city we stopped for gas. Dad
had left a map and directions on the dashboard of
the car, so now I knew where we were going: 1200
Bayside Street.

Well, I was pretty desperate, so for the first time ever I used my Ladybug.

I finished my call right before Dad came back to the car, and we headed into the city. I just wish I took a better look at that map, because when we pulled up to Bayside Street, I realized it was the parking lot for the baseball stadium. But by then it was too late.

It turns out Mom had bought us tickets to the baseball game for some special father-son bonding and Dad was trying to keep it a surprise.

But it took Dad a long time to explain all of that to the cops. After he cleared things up with the police, Dad wasn't in the mood for a baseball game, so he just took me home.

I felt kind of bad because the seats Mom got us were in the third row, and it looked to me like they cost a fortune.

Tuesday

I finally found out what that phone call was all about the other day. Dad had been on the phone with Gramma, and they were talking about Sweetie, not me.

Mom and Dad had decided to give the dog to Gramma, and Dad dropped Sweetie off on Sunday night. To be honest with you, I don't think anyone's really gonna miss him around here.

Me and Dad haven't talked to each other since then, and I've been looking for excuses to stay out of the house. I found a really good one yesterday. There was a commercial on TV for this store called the Game Hut, which is where I buy all my video games.

They're having a competition where you play at your local store, and if you win you get to advance to the national playoffs. And the winner of THAT gets a million bucks.

The competition at my local store is on Saturday. I'm sure there are gonna be a ton of people at that thing, so I'm gonna go super early to make sure I get a good place in line.

I learned that trick from Rodrick. Whenever he wants to get tickets to a concert, he camps out the night before. In fact, that's where he met his band's lead singer, Bill.

Rowley and his dad go camping all the time, so I knew he had a tent. I called Rowley and told him about the video game contest and how we could win a million bucks.

But Rowley was acting nervous on the phone. I think he was still worried that I had electrical superpowers or something, and the only way to get him to calm down was to promise I wouldn't use them on him.

Even after we were past that, Rowley didn't seem comfortable with the campout idea. He said his mom and dad banned him from seeing me for the rest of the summer.

I pretty much figured that, but I had a plan to get around it. I told Rowley that I'd tell my parents I was going up to his house to spend the night, and he could tell his parents he was going to Collin's.

Rowley STILL didn't seem sure, so I told him
I'd bring him his very own box of gummy bears if
he came along, and that sold him.

Saturday
Last night we met at the top of the hill at 9:00.
Rowley brought the camping equipment and the
sleeping bag, and I brought the flashlight and
some chocolate energy bars.

I didn't have the gummy bears right at that
moment, but I promised Rowley I'd buy him some
the first chance I got.

When we got to the Game Hut we were the only
people there, and I couldn't believe our luck.

So we pitched our tent in front of the store
before anyone else could take our spot.

Then we watched the door to make sure no one
tried to cut in front of us.

I figured the best way to save our place in line
was to sleep in shifts. I even offered to take
the first shift and let Rowley sleep, because
that's just the kind of person I am.

After my shift was over I woke Rowley up for his turn, but he fell back asleep in about five seconds. So I shook him awake and told him he needed to stay alert.

Rowley didn't even bother trying to defend himself.

I decided it was up to ME to make sure nobody got in front of us, so I stayed up all night. I was starting to have trouble keeping my eyes open around 9:00 in the morning, and I ate both of the energy bars I packed to keep myself going.

I got chocolate all over my hands, and that gave me an idea. I opened the tent flap, then slipped my hand inside and made it crawl like a spider.

I thought it would be funny to make Rowley think it was the muddy hand. I didn't hear any noises coming from inside the tent, so I thought Rowley was still sleeping. But before I had a chance to open the flap and check, my hand got crushed to smithereens.

I pulled my hand out of the tent, and my thumb was already starting to turn purple.

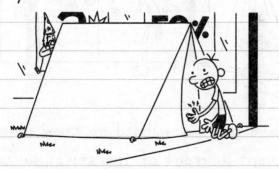

I was really ticked off at Rowley. Not because he smashed my hand with a mallet, but because he thought that it could stop the muddy hand.

Any fool knows you have to either use fire or acid to stop a muddy hand. All a mallet's gonna do is make it angry.

I was about to give Rowley a piece of my mind, but right then the guy from the Game Hut came and opened the front door. I tried to ignore the throbbing pain in my thumb and focus on the reason we came here.

The Game Hut guy wanted to know why we had a tent in front of the store, so I told him we were there to compete in the video game contest. But he didn't even know what I was talking about.

So I had to show him the poster from the window
to get him up to speed.

The clerk said the store wasn't really set up for
a video game tournament but since there were
only two of us, maybe we could just play each
other in the back room.

I was a little irritated at first, but then I realized
all I needed to do to win this tournament was to
beat Rowley. So the clerk set us up to play a
death match in Twisted Wizard. I almost felt
sorry for Rowley, because I'm pretty much an
expert at that game. But when we started to
play, I realized my thumb was so messed up I
couldn't press the buttons on the controller.

All I could do was run around in circles while
Rowley shot me over and over.

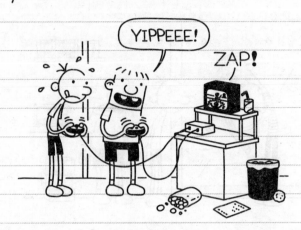

Rowley ended up beating me 15-0. The clerk
told Rowley he won the competition and had a
choice: He could either fill out the paperwork to
go to the national tournament, or he could get a
giant box of chocolate-covered raisins.

I'll bet you can guess which one Rowley picked.

<u>Sunday</u>

You know, I should have just stuck with my
original plan and stayed inside this summer,
because all my trouble started the minute I
stepped out of the house.

I haven't seen Rowley since he stole that video
game competition from me, and Dad hasn't spoken
to me since I almost got him arrested.

But I think things started to turn around for
me and Dad today. You remember that article
about how "Li'l Cutie" was being passed on from
the father to his son?

Well, the son's first comic came out in the paper
today, and it looks like the new "Li'l Cutie" is
gonna be even worse than the original.

Daddy, can you make my hiccups hic-DOWN?

I showed Dad, and he agreed with me.

That's when I realized things are gonna be OK between the two of us. Me and Dad might not agree on everything, but at least we agree on the important stuff.

I guess some people would say that hating a comic is a pretty flimsy foundation for a relationship, but the truth is me and Dad hate LOTS of the same things.

Me and Dad might not have one of those close father-son relationships, but that's fine with me. I've learned that there is such a thing as TOO close.

I realized vacation was pretty much over when Mom finished up with her photo album today. I flipped through it, and to be honest with you, I don't think it was a very accurate record of our summer. But I guess the person who takes the pictures is the one who gets to tell the story.

"Best Summer Ever!"

READING IS FUN

The "Reading Is Fun" gang says "no" to video games.

Now Gregory can't stop reading!

SQUIRREL-BOY FOUND LIVING IN CENTRAL PARK

Gregory plays a game of hide 'n' seek with a summer pal.

"Just what I wanted!"

Three generations of Heffley men bond over brunch.

Rodrick says, "Who needs the beach?"

A magical Fourth of July.

Splish, splash!
Gregory has a blast
at the pool.

Oops! Mom gets in
the picture.

Gregory feels "cool"
hanging out with
a lifeguard pal.

Best friends!

ACKNOWLEDGMENTS

Thanks to all the fans of the *Wimpy Kid* series for inspiring and motivating me to write these stories. Thanks to all of the booksellers across the nation for putting my books in kids' hands.

Thanks to my family for all the love and support. It's been fun to share this experience with you.

Thanks to the folks at Abrams for working hard to make sure this book happened. A special thanks to Charlie Kochman, my editor; Jason Wells, my publicist; and Scott Auerbach, managing editor extraordinaire.

Thanks to everyone in Hollywood for working so hard to bring Greg Heffley to life, especially Nina, Brad, Carla, Riley, Elizabeth, and Thor. And thanks, Sylvie and Keith, for your help and guidance.

ABOUT THE AUTHOR

Jeff Kinney is an online game developer and designer, and a #1 *New York Times* bestselling author. In 2009, Jeff was named one of *Time* magazine's 100 Most Influential People in the World. He spent his childhood in the Washington D.C.area and moved to New England in 1995. Jeff lives in southern Massachusetts with his wife and their two sons.

望子快乐

朱子庆

在一个人的一生中，"与有荣焉"的机会或有，但肯定不多。因为儿子译了一部畅销书，而老爸被邀涂鸦几句，像这样的与荣，我想，即使放眼天下，也没有几人领得吧。

儿子接活儿翻译《小屁孩日记》时，还在读着大三。这是安安他第一次领译书稿，多少有点紧张和兴奋吧，起初他每译几段，便飞鸽传书，不一会儿人也跟过来，在我面前"项庄舞剑"地问："有意思么？有意思么？"怎么当时我就没有作乐不可支状呢？于今想来，我竟很有些后悔。对于一个喂饱段子与小品的中国人，若说还有什么洋幽默能令我们"绝倒"，难！不过，当安安译成杀青之时，图文并茂，我得以从头到尾再读一遍，我得说，这部书岂止有意思呢，读了它使我有一种冲动，假如时间可以倒流，我很想尝试重新做一回父亲！我不免窃想，安安在译它的时候，不知会怎样腹诽我这个老爸呢！

我宁愿儿子是书里那个小屁孩！

你可能会说，你别是在做秀吧，小屁孩格雷将来能出息成个什么样子，实在还很难说……这个质疑，典型地出诸一个中国人之口，出之于为父母的中国人之口。望子成龙，一定要孩子出息成个什么样子，虽说初衷也是为了孩子，但最终却是苦了孩子。"生年不满百，常怀千岁忧。"现在，由于这深重的忧患，我们已经把成功学启示的模式都做到胎教了！而望子快乐，有谁想过？从小就快乐，快乐一生？惭愧，我也是看了《小屁孩日记》才想到这点，然而儿子已不再年少！我觉得很有些对不住儿子！

我从来没有对安安的"少年老成"感到过有什么不妥，毕竟少年老成使人放心。而今读其译作而被触动，此心才为之不安起来。我在想，比起美国的小屁孩格雷和他的同学们，我们中国的小屁孩们是不是活得不很小屁孩？是不是普遍地过于负重、乏乐和少年老成？而当他们将来长大，娶妻（嫁夫）生子（女），为人父母，会不会还要循此逻辑再造下一代？想想安安少年时，起早贪黑地读书、写作业，小四眼，十足一个书呆子，类似格雷那样的调皮、贪玩、小有恶搞、缰绳牢笼不住地敢于尝试和行动主义……太缺少了。印象中，安安最突出的一次，也就是读小学三年级时，做了一回带头大哥，拔了校园里所有自行车的气门芯并四处派发，仅此而已吧（此处请在家长指导下阅读）。

说点别的吧。中国作家写的儿童文学作品，很少能引发成年读者的阅读兴趣。安徒生童话之所以风靡天下，在于它征服了成年读者。在我看来，《小屁孩日记》也属于成人少年兼宜的读物，可以父子同修！谁没有年少轻狂？谁没有豆蔻年华？只不过呢，对于为父母者，阅读它，会使你由会心一笑而再笑，继以感慨系之，进而不免有所自省，对照和检讨一下自己和孩子的关系，以及在某些类似事情的处理上，自己是否欠妥？等等。它虽系成人所作，书中对孩子心性的把握，却准确传神；虽非心理学著作，对了解孩子的心理和行为，也不无参悟和启示。品学兼优和顽劣不学的孩子毕竟是少数，小屁孩格雷是"中间人物"的一个玲珑典型，着实招人怜爱——在格雷身上，有着我们彼此都难免有的各样小心思、小算计、小毛病，就好像阿Q，读来透着与我们有那么一种割不断的血缘关系，这，也许就是此书在美国乃至全球都特别畅销的原因吧！

　　最后我想申明的是，第一读者身份在我是弥足珍惜的，因为，宝贝儿子出生时，第一眼看见他的是医生，老爸都摊不上第一读者呢！

我眼中的 ……

好书，爱不释手！

★ 王汐子（女，19 岁，2009 年留学美国，攻读大学传媒专业）《小屁孩日记》在美国掀起的阅读风潮可不是盖的，在我留学美国的这一年中，不止一次目睹这套书对太平洋彼岸人民的巨大影响。高速公路上巨大的广告宣传牌就不用说了，我甚至在学校书店买课本时看到了这套书被大大咧咧地摆上书架，"小屁孩"的搞笑日记就这样理直气壮地充当起了美国大学生的课本教材！为什么这套书如此受欢迎？为什么一个普普通通的小男孩能让这么多成年人捧腹大笑？也许可以套用一个万能句式"每个人心中都有一个XXX"。每个人心中都有一个小屁孩，每个人小时候也有过这样的时光，每天都有点鸡毛蒜皮的小烦恼，像作业这么多怎么办啦，要考试了书都没有看怎么办啦……但是大部分时候还是因为调皮捣乱被妈妈教训……就这样迷迷糊糊地走过了"小屁孩"时光，等长大后和朋友们讨论后才恍然大悟，随即不禁感慨，原来那时候我们都一样呀……是呀，全世界的小屁孩都一样！

★ 读者 书山有径（发表于 2010－01－31）这是一本真正写给孩子的书。作为圣诞礼物买给女儿，由于作业多，平时只能睡前读几页。放假了，女儿天天捧着这本书，一天到晚为书的人和事笑个不停；天天给我讲鬼屋的故事，用神秘而恐怖的语气。并且，天天问我，生活中她的朋友哪些应该被叫做"小屁孩"，怎么个"屁"法。

★ 读者 zhizhimother（发表于 2009 - 06 - 12）在杂志上看到这书的介绍，一时冲动在当当上下了单，没想到，一买回来一家人抢着看，笑得前仰后合。我跟女儿一人抢到一本，老公很不满意，他嘟囔着下一本出的时候他要第一个看。看多了面孔雷同的好孩子的书，看到这本，真是深有感触，我们的孩子其实都是这样长大的～～

轻松阅读 捧腹大笑

★ 这是著名的畅销书作家小巫的儿子 Sam 口述的英语和中文读后感：I like *Diary of a Wimpy Kid* because Greg is an average child just like us. His words are really funny and the illustrations are hilarious. His stories are eventful and most of them involve silliness. 我喜欢《小屁孩日记》，因为 Greg 是跟我们一样的普通孩子。他的故事很好玩儿，令我捧腹大笑，他做的事情很搞笑，有点儿傻呼呼的。书里的插图也很幽默。

★ 读者 bnulizi（发表于 2009 - 06 - 08）同学在开心网里转帖推荐这套书，于是我便傻傻地买了一套。看后发现还是挺赞的，笑料很多啊。而且最精彩的地方往往都是通过一段文字后的那幅图来表达的，我笑到肚子痛……

★ 读者 dearm 暖 baby（发表于 2009 - 07 - 29）我 12 岁了，过生日时妈妈给我买了这样两本书，真的很有趣！一半是中文，一半是英文，彻底打破了"英文看不懂看下面中文"的局限！而且这本书彻底地给我来了次大放松，"重点中学"的压力也一扫而光！总之，两个字：超赞！

★ 读者 mei298（发表于 2010 - 01 - 23）儿子超喜欢，边看边

大笑。买了1~4册，没几天就看完了，特别喜欢那一段"弗雷格跟我在同一个班上体育课，他的语言自成一家，比如说他要去厕所的时候，他就说——果汁！果汁！！！我们已经大致清楚弗雷格那套了，不过我看老师们大概还没弄懂。老师说——好吧，小伙子……你可真难伺候！还端来了一杯汽水。"为了这段话，儿子笑了一整天，到睡觉的时候想想还笑。

孩子爱上写日记了！

★ 读者 pinganfurong（发表于 2009 – 11 – 10）一直想让九岁的儿子记记日记，但始终不喜欢给他"布置任务"。生活啦、工作啦、学习啦、休闲啦、娱乐啦等等等等，都是自己的事，自己喜欢，才能做好。写文章、记日记，也是如此。给老师写，为爹妈记，是件很烦人的事。命题作文、任务日记，只会让孩子讨厌写作文，讨厌记日记。讨厌的事能干好？笑话！怎么办呢？怎样才能让儿子自觉自愿地喜欢上记日记呢？于是，给儿子买了《小屁孩日记》。果不其然，儿子读完后，便拉着我去给他买回一个又大又厚的日记本，兴趣盎然地记起日记来。

★ 读者 ddian2003（发表于 2009 – 12 – 22）正是于丹的那几句话吸引我买下了这套书。自己倒没看，但女儿却用了三天学校的课余时间就看完了，随后她大受启发，连着几天都写了日记。现在这书暂时搁在书柜里，已和女儿约定，等她学了英文后再来看一遍，当然要看书里的英文了。所以这书还是买得物有所值的。毕竟女儿喜欢！！

做个"不听话的好孩子"

★ 读者 水真爽（发表于 2010 – 03 – 27）这套书是买给我上小学二年级的儿子的。有时候他因为到该读书的时间而被要求从网游下来很恼火。尽管带着气，甚至眼泪，可是读起这本书来，总是能被书中小屁孩的种种淘气出格行为和想法弄得哈哈大笑。书中的卡通漫画也非常不错。这种文字漫画形式的日记非常具有趣味性，老少咸宜。对低年级孩子或爱画漫画的孩子尤其有启发作用。更重要的是提醒家长们好好留意观察这些"不怎么听话"的小屁孩们的内心世界，他们的健康成长需要成人的呵护引导，但千万不要把他们都变成只会"听大人话"的好孩子。

★ 读者 寂寞朱丽叶（发表于 2009 - 06 - 10）最近我身边的朋友都在看这本书，出于好奇我也买了一套，美国"囧男孩"格雷满脑子的鬼主意，虽然不是人们心目中好孩子的形象，但很真实，我很喜欢他，还有点羡慕他，我怎么没有他有趣呢。

对照《小屁孩日记》分享育儿体验

★ 读者 gjrzj2002@＊＊＊.＊＊＊（发表于 2010 - 05 - 21）看完四册书，我想着自己虽然不可能有三个孩子，但一个孩子的成长经历至今仍记忆犹新。儿子还是幼儿的时候，比较像曼尼，在爸妈眼中少有缺点，真是让人越看越爱，想要什么就基本上能得到什么。整个幼儿期父母对孩子肯定大过否定。上了小学，儿子的境地就不怎么从容了，上学的压力时时处处在影响着他，小家伙要承受各方面的压力，父母、老师、同学，太过我行我素、大而化之都是行不通的，比如没写作业的话，老师、家长的批评和提醒是少不了的，孩子在慢慢学着适应这种生活，烦恼也随之而来，这一阶段比较像格雷，虽然儿子的思维还没那么丰富，快乐和烦恼的花样都没那么多，但处境差不多，表扬和赞美不像以前那样轻易就能得到了。儿子青年时代会是什么样子我还不得而知，也不可想象，那种水到渠成的阶段要靠前面的积累，我希望自己到时候能平心静气，坦然接受，无论儿子成长成什么样子。

气味相投的好伙伴

★ 上海市外国语大学附属第一实验中学，中预 10 班，沈昕仪 Elaine：《小屁孩日记》读来十分轻松。虽然没有用十分华丽的语言，却使我感受到了小屁孩那缤纷多彩的生活，给我带来无限的欢乐。那精彩的插图、幽默的文字实在是太有趣了，当中的故事在我们身边都有可能发生，让人身临其境。格雷总能说出我的心里话，他是和我有着共同语言的朋友。所以他们搞的恶作剧一直让我跃跃欲试，也想找一次机会尝试一下。不知别的读者怎么想，我觉得格雷挺喜欢出风头的。我也是这样的人，总怕别人无视了自己。当看到格雷蹦出那些稀奇古怪的点子的时候，我多想帮他一把啊——毕竟我们是"气味相投"的同类人嘛。另一方面，我身处在外语学校，时刻都需要积累英语单词，但这件事总是让我觉得枯燥乏味。而《小屁孩日记》帮了我的大忙：我在享受快乐阅读的同时，还可以对照中英文学到很多常用英语单词。我发现其实生活中还有很多事情值得我们去用笔写下来。即使是小事，这些童年的故事也是很值得我们回忆的。既然还生活在童年，还能够写下那些故事，又何乐而不为呢？

亲爱的读者，你看完这本书后，有什么感想吗？请来电话或是登录本书的博客与我们分享吧！等本书再版时，这里也许换上了你的读后感呢！

我们的电话号码是 020－83795744，博客地址是：blog. sina. com. cn/ wimpykid。

悦读"小·屁孩"

《小·屁孩日记①——鬼屋创意》

在日记里，格雷记叙了他如何驾驭充满冒险
的中学生活，如何巧妙逃脱学校歌唱比赛，最重
要的是如何不让任何人发现他的秘密。他经常想
捉弄人反被人捉弄；他常常想做好事却弄巧成
拙；他屡屡身陷尴尬境遇竟逢"凶"化吉。他不
是好孩子，也不是坏孩子，就只是普通的孩子；
他有点自私，但重要关头也会挺身而出保护朋友……

《小·屁孩日记②——谁动了千年奶酪》

在《小·屁孩日记②》里，主人公格雷度过一个
没有任何奇迹发生的圣诞节。为打发漫长无聊的
下雪天，他和死党罗利雄心勃勃地想要堆出"世
界上最大的雪人"，却因为惹怒老爸，雪人被销
毁；格雷可是不甘寂寞的，没几天，他又找到乐
子了，在送幼儿园小朋友过街的时候，他制造了
一起"虫子事件"吓唬小朋友，并嫁祸罗利，从而
导致一场"严重"的友情危机……格雷能顺利化解
危机，重新赢得好朋友罗利的信任吗？

《小·屁孩日记③——好孩子不撒谎》

在本册里，格雷开始了他的暑假生活。慢
着，别以为他的假期会轻松愉快。其实他整个暑

假都被游泳训练班给毁了。他还自作聪明地导演了一出把同学齐拉格当成隐形人的闹剧，他以为神不知鬼不觉就可以每天偷吃姜饼，终于在圣诞前夜东窗事发，付出了巨大的代价……

《小·屁孩日记④——偷鸡不成蚀把米》

本集里，格雷仿佛落入了他哥哥罗德里克的魔掌中一般，怎么也逃脱不了厄运：他在老妈的威逼利诱下跟罗德里克学爵士鼓，却只能在一旁干看罗德里克自娱自乐；与好友罗利一起偷看罗德里克窝藏的鬼片，却不幸玩过火害罗利受伤，为此格雷不得不付出惨重代价——代替罗利在全校晚会上表演魔术——而他的全部表演内容就是为一个一年级小朋友递魔术道具。更大的悲剧还在后面，他不惜花"重金"购买罗德里克的旧作业想要蒙混过关，却不幸买到一份不及格的作业。最后，他暑假误入女厕所的囧事还被罗德里克在全校大肆宣扬……格雷还有脸在学校混吗？他的日记还能继续下去吗？

《小·屁孩日记⑤——午餐零食大盗》

格雷在新的一年里展开了他的学校生活：克雷格老师的词典不翼而飞，于是每天课间休息时所有同学都被禁止外出，直至字典被找到；格雷的午餐零食从糖果变成了两个水果，他怀疑是哥哥罗德里克偷了零食，誓要查出真相。因为午餐零食闹的"糖荒"，让格雷精神不振，总是在下午的课堂上打瞌睡。格雷没有多余的零用钱，不能自己买糖果，于是他想到了自己埋下的时光宝盒——里面放着三美元的钞票。格雷挖出时光宝盒，暂时缓解了"糖荒"。另一边厢，学校即将举行第一次的情人节舞会。格雷对漂亮的同班同学荷莉心仪已久，就决定趁舞会好好表现。在舞会上，他成功与荷莉互相交换了情人节卡片，并想邀请荷莉跳舞，于是他向人群中的荷莉走去……

《小·屁孩日记⑥——可怕的炮兵学校》

格雷想尽一切办法让老爸摆脱一些可怕的念头。格雷的老爸一直希望他能加强锻炼，就让他加入了周末的足球队。格雷在足球队吃尽了苦头：他先被教练派去当球童，在荆棘丛里捡球累了个半死；然后又被要求坐在寒风中观赛，冷得他直打哆嗦；后来他自以为聪明地选择了后备守门员的位置，最后却因为正选守门员受伤而不得不披挂上阵。在输掉足球比赛后，格雷觉得老爸因此而生气了。未想老爸又冒出另一个更可怕的念头：把格雷送进炮兵学校。格雷却自动请缨加入周末的童子军，因为这样一来他就不必再去参加足球训练了。然而，在童子军的父子营中，格雷又为老爸惹来麻烦……老爸决定在这个学期结束后，就立刻把格雷送进炮兵学校。眼看暑假就要开始了，格雷因此坐立不安……

《小·屁孩日记⑦——从天而降的巨债》

暑假刚开始，格雷就与老爸老妈展开了拉锯战：老爸老妈坚持认为孩子放暑假就应该到户外去活动，但格雷却宁愿躲在家里打游戏机、看肥皂剧。不得已之下，格雷跟着死党罗利到乡村俱乐部玩，两人在那儿吃了一点东西，就欠下了83美元的"巨债"。于是，他们不得不想尽一切办法打工还债……

他们能把债务还清吗？格雷又惹出了什么笑话？

《小屁孩日记⑧——"头盖骨摇晃机"的幸存者》

老妈带全家上了旅行车，看到防晒霜和泳衣，格雷满心以为是去海滩度假，却原来只是去水上乐园——一个令格雷吃过很多苦头的地方，过去的不愉快记忆也就罢了，这次好不容易做好一切准备，广播却通知"因闪电天气停止营业"；回到家里又怎样呢？格雷发现他心爱的鱼惨遭罗德里克宠物鱼的"毒口"；盼望已久的小狗阿甜来了，非但不是补偿，反而使格雷的生活一团糟；格雷发现救生员是希尔斯小姐，这使得他一改对于小镇游泳场的糟糕看法，小心眼儿活动起来；妈妈安排了一个格雷与爸爸改善关系的机会，可是格雷却用"甲壳虫小姐"召来了警察，搞得老爸灰溜溜的，他们关系更僵；老妈处心积虑安排格雷和死党罗利的一家去了海滩，格雷却又惹了祸……

我们可爱又倒霉的格雷啊，他该如何处理这一切？"头盖骨摇晃机"又是怎么回事？